The Knights of Royal Pond

by

Gordon Goodman

ISBN: 0-9746027-7-9

DEDICATION

This book is dedicated to all those who feel less than enough. Nobody's magic is better than your own.

CONTENTS

i

ACKNOWLEDGMENTS

I want to thank Tom Hatten, who, among many other things, had a children's television show when I was a small child. Years later he became a friend. His show taught me about creativity. More than that, it did me the great favor of teaching me that mistakes are simply things waiting to find their true identity.

PROLOGUE

There is a pond which lies at the very center of a world invisible to humans. It is not that humans cannot see it. It is merely that they cannot understand what they see. So, like most things humans do not understand, they pretend it is not there. Yet, there was a time, not long ago, when this invisible world nearly destroyed human kind, and animal kind, and fish kind, and bird, and insect, and all life on this blue marble of a world.

Most humans will never know of the danger that once threatened the world, because they do not understand the language.

But you are young. And you may still know of this tale if you listen closely. For it is not the language of man that you must learn.

It is the language...of frogs.

CHAPTER ONE

A voice, an unsure voice, sang to a twangy guitar. The voice came from a tiny boat, holding two mice. The male mouse, in a leather jerkin, was standing in the boat singing to a girl mouse, who was relaxing comfortably at one end.

WHEN THE MOON IS HANGING HIGH
AND SILVER STARS FILL UP THE SKY
I WONDER HOW SOMEONE LIKE I
FOUND SOMEONE LIKE YOU...

WHEN THE NIGHT IS SOFT AND STILL
AND BREEZES FLOAT ACROSS THE HILL
NO DREAM BECOMES A DREAM UNTIL
IT FINDS SOMEONE LIKE YOU...

I COULD SAIL ACROSS THE SEVEN SEAS
FIGHT GIANTS THAT ARE TALL AS TREES
CLIMB MOUNTAINS THAT ARE MADE OF
CHEESE…

NO OTHER DREAM COULD BE
HALF AS REAL FOR ME
CAUSE I FOUND A DREAM COME TRUE
WHEN I FOUND SOMEONE LIKE YOU.....

He broke off the song because the tiny boat was rocking. He stared down into the dark water.

"Could be anything in there," he thought. "Could be a big fish. Big enough to swallow us up. Could be a water snake, or a beaver. Or maybe a monster that only comes out once every hundred years..."

"Don't stop," the girl mouse, named Alice, said as she stretched her two furry little arms. "Isn't this romantic, Jeremy? The moon. The pond. The music."

Jeremy shivered. "Yeah, the owls, the wild dogs, and whatever lives under this water, "

"Oh, don't start that again? What are you? A big 'scaredy cat'?"

"Ooh," whispered Jeremy, "I forgot to mention cats..."

"Jeremy, if you don't feel like you can protect me, then maybe I should just go back and find someone who can."

"No, no, I didn't say that, Alice...not exactly. It's just that, it's night, and we might not find our way back, that's all..."

Jeremy reached in back of him and awkwardly tried to swat at something. It was his tail. It was quivering violently. It always did that when he got scared. He tried to push it down so Alice wouldn't notice.

"Ooh, look!" Alice said, sitting up in the boat. "What's that light over there?" She was pointing to a light coming through the reeds near shore. "Lets go over there, okay?"

"Alice, we don't know what might be over there. It could be something with big teeth, or big claws, or big feet..."

"Ugh!" Alice moaned, "what IS it with you? You just have no sense of adventure at all!"

With these very words, three black shapes appeared out of the darkness and flitted in front of the bright yellow moon hanging just over Alice's head. Three sets of yellow eyes hovered around the pink bow between Alice's ears. She continued complaining, which was what Alice did best...

"I'm not afraid, and I'm a GIRL! I'm SUPPOSED to be afraid. You're supposed to be brave!"

Over each of Alice's shoulders, moonlight shone on the hideous little faces floating in the air. They were bats. Jeremy was petrified.

As Alice jabbered on, they began to make faces at Jeremy, their tiny sharp teeth flashing as they imitated Alice's every gesture. Jeremy's tail was quivering uncontrollably. He pointed at the shapes.

"A-A-A-A-A-Alice..."

"...I asked you to bring me here," said Alice, not about to be interrupted, "because I thought it might be fun! But here we are, a great night out on the pond...in a boat...with the stars...AND the moon, and look at you! Look at your tail! You're scared for no reason at all! Just like always!"

"Buh-buh-buh-buh...." Jeremy stuttered and pointed at the bats behind Alice's head. She turned and looked. The instant she turned, the bats disappeared.

"Right! I thought so! Augh! What am I doing here! I'm young! I'm pretty! I want some excitement! Some fun! Is that too much to ask!"

The bats reappeared and resumed making faces at Jeremy. Alice hadn't complained in an hour or two. So she'd been storing up.

"Other boyfriends are wild and brave and romantic! But being with you is like being with my grandfather! I have a reputation to think of, you know? I mean, all my friends think I'm gorgeous and always ask me why I go out with YOU."

Even bats can only take so much complaining in one night, so two of the bats took off into the darkness. The third bat lingered, flitting over to sit on Jeremy's shoulder. He was too frightened to move. The bat whispered into Jeremy's ear. It spoke with a breathy Mexican accent.

"Women... hee hee... can't live WITH 'em... but you chure' can live great WITHOUT 'em. Eh Hermano?"

Jeremy couldn't stand it anymore. He shook his shoulders and flailed his arms.

"Wuh-wuh-wuh-we gotta go home now, Alice!"

"Are you even listening to me, Jeremy?" Alice said, too busy ranting to notice the bat flying away. "You see? You just don't respect my opinions. Dozens of boys would listen to me for hours, I'll bet. All I want is what I deserve. I mean, what good is it being better looking than everybody else if people don't treat you like you're special? Huh? Give you presents? Tell you how beautiful you are and how they don't deserve to be around you? I AM beautiful, right? RIGHT?"

Jeremy nodded frantically as he grabbed for the oars.

"So, all I want is what I've got coming to me. All I want is to be adored. I don't think that's very much to ask. And I can find plenty of people who adore me if you don't." Satisfied with her logic, Alice sat back, crossed her arms and pouted.

Jeremy started rowing to shore, feeling better and better the closer he came to home.

CHAPTER TWO

At the other end of the same pond, a dark shadow disturbed the reflection that the moon had painted on the water.

The shadow was in the shape of a duck.

The duck paddled slowly, mumbling to herself with her head bowed low to the glistening water. She was remembering something, and the scene seemed to be playing over and over in the flickering ripples beneath her...

The afternoon sun was melting as Maggie, a dirty gray duck, swam across a small bay framed in reeds. As she passed the wall of reeds, she found herself in view of a gaggle of other ducks, all splashing, and diving, and talking so loudly they must have thought there was no one else in the entire pond but them.

Maggie tried to swim by without them noticing her, but it was too late.

"Hey! Look who's sneakin' up on us!" one duck shouted to the others.

"Oh no!" another one called, "It's the old hag! Don't look boys 'er we'll all git' turned ta' stone!"

"Why, that's the ugliest dang'd duck in the whole wide world," shouted yet another duck, this one with a long red beak that made him look like he had a cold. His name was Honk, and he must indeed have had a cold, since he immediately sneezed and flipped himself backwards into the water.

The gaggle of ducks began to spread out in a semi-circle, jeering at Maggie and splashing water at her.

A duck, named Duke, who seemed to be their leader, floated out of the semi-circle to face Maggie.

"Fella's...fella's...," Duke said, spreading his wings to calm them down, "where's your hospitality? We're all ducks 'roun' here. We're all equals. Just cause Maggie here, don't got much in the looks department, don't mean she ain't one of us.....Why shore...don't mean we cain't act like ourselves. All friendly like."

At this the other ducks were confused.

They WERE being themselves. In fact, being rude and awful was what they did the best. Duke went on.

"We was jest talkin' about, uhm... 'bout how we was gonna go about doin' somethin'."

"Doin' what?" Maggie asked nervously, trying to keep as much distance as she could from the others. The semi-circle of ducks had tightened. There was no room to fly away now.

"Well, uh,... settin' a trap!" Duke went on. "Yeah, that's it! Now, idn't that sumpthin"! I'm so fergitful, sometimes, if'n I couldn't see myself in the water I think I'd even fergit I was here! Now I ask ya', ain't that just pitiful?"

"Shore is," Honk spoke up, trying to be one of the gang.

"Shut up!" Duke snapped. "Who asked you anyways."

"Well, YOU did," said Honk. "You said, idn't that pitiful an'...an'...ahhh...ahhh...AH CHOO!" and he went flying backwards into the water once more. Another duck, named, 'Streak', cut in.

"...the 'Mud Hawk,' right? Is that what you mean?"

Duke looked over at Streak and suddenly caught on. With a nod of thanks, Duke continued.

"Yeah, 'course," said Duke, "that's it, a trap fer' the Mud Hawk, that was what we was talkin' about, 'for I was so rudely interrupted." And he gave Honk a smack on the back of the head with his wing. This sent Honk into the water face-first this time with a "SPLASH!"

Streak swam in closer to Maggie.

"Ya' see," Streak whispered confidentially, "the Mud Hawk's this big ole' hawk that flies around with big ole' claws full of oats and corn and..."

"And melons and peaches . . .," called another duck.

"And blackberries, and blueberries...," chimed in another. They were all catching on the game now.

"An' ENTIRE big ole' apple trees. An' entire ole' peach trees an' ..."

"SMACK!" went a wing, as it collided with the back of Honk's head. Down into the water the red-beaked duck went again.

"Id'jit," growled Duke.   "...see,"   Duke continued, "all we gotta do is lure it down to the ground, like."

"How do you do that?" Maggie asked.

The Leader narrowed his shifty orange eyes and

glanced at his gang of ducks.

"Well...we been thinkin' about what the Mud Hawk loves more'n anything in this whole danged world..." Everyone edged in closer so they could hear. "More'n anything else in the whole universe, the Mud Hawk loves....MUD!"

"It does?" Maggie asked.

"It does?" asked Honk, sneezing again. This was a big sneeze, and it sent him spinning backwards three or four times.

Duke could see Maggie was curious now. He wanted to keep her interested. He nudged Streak to continue with the story for him.

"Uh, yeah," said Streak. "...that's 'cause it... so's it c'n uh...so's it can hide all the stuff it carries around."

"Yeah, that's right," continued a duck called Rufus. "So if we can get the Mud Hawk ta' come down here, and have it bury all the things its been heftin' around, well then, we can go over later and dig it all up. We can eat till we bust, I'll betcha..."

The other ducks agreed by slapping their wings on the water. They all loved this cruel game.

"Yup," went on Duke, "a Sunday-go-to-meetin' feast. Hoo-doggies!"

"All you kin eat!!" offered Streak.

Somehow Honk had gotten in back of everybody, but they still heard his voice.

"Entire big ole' watermelons an'--"

In unison, the gaggle of ducks turned and splashed Honk with as much water as their wings could scoop.

Honk almost drowned.

"COUGH", "COUGH", okay, fergit the melons too. I'm jest tryin' ta' help doggone it!" he shouted.

Maggie wanted to get back to the Mud Hawk.

"So...how do we get it to come down here?"

"Now we was just havin' that intellekshull discussion when you came by," said Duke, very seriously as he put a wing over Maggie's back. No one ever got this close to Maggie, so it made her uncomfortable, but she was so curious about the Mud Hawk she ignored the uncomfortable feeling.

"See, what we need is, fer somebody ta' go over there to the edge of the pond over yonder, 'n roll around a little in the mud. You know, right out in the moonlight? The sight of fresh mud's jest too good for a Mud Hawk to pass up, you c'n take my word fer' that." All the other ducks nodded their heads heartily while giving each other sly sideward glances.

"Somebody out there a'rollin' aroun', havin' fun, makes the mud awful appealin' ta' that ole' boy, the Mud Hawk."

"You sure it doesn't, "gulp", eat ducks?"

"No! Now...now you don't think we'd do anythin' dangerous, do ya? The Mud Hawk don't eat meat. No! That ain't our problem. Our problem seems ta' be our natural good looks, ya' see. Now, WE can't be the ones ta' roll in the mud on account o' our markin's and our strikin' appearance. That'd tip off the Mud Hawk fer shore. But YOU, why you're almost the color o' mud right now, see..."

"You'd be perfect!" Streak whispered.

"What the doctor ordered!" said Rufus.

"Got that one right!" said Honk who had surfaced just beside them, "gol' dang'd absolutely, bee-ond a doubt, without question--"

"WHAP" came a wing and Honk was knocked forward into the water. He came up sputtering, "Now come on! Dang it! What was wrong with that!" The ducks squished together and squeezed Honk out of the circle.

"Well?" asked the Leader.

"Think of them melons," whispered Streak.

"And the oats and peaches," said Rufus.

"Berries," said one duck.

"Sweets," said another.

"An' ENTIRE OLE'--"

This time the five or six ducks turned around and battered Honk with their wings until he disappeared under the water.

"Well, if you're sure it'll work," Maggie said. "What do I have to do?"

Duke smiled victoriously. The moon was starting to peek over the ridge. He pointed to shore.

"There's the best mud on the whole pond, I'll betcha. Just go right over there an' roll around in that soft warm mud, jest relaxin' and slippin' around 'til he comes down."

"But it's night. How's he gonna see me?"

"Oh, well, they see best by moonlight," Duke assured her.

"Why, I'll bet he could see a spot o' mud a thousand feet away in the moonlight. But we want him ta' come down ta' <u>this</u> one. An you're jest about the only'est one who c'n do it. All ya' have ta' do is go on over there, roll around in the mud a little 'n we'll jes' be waitin' behind the reeds here." He gave Maggie a little nudge and she started to move slowly over to the edge of the pond, looking back occasionally for assurance. The ducks all motioned her on with waving wings and sincere smiles.

Honk emerged from the water, dizzy and batting away stars that were spinning all around him.

"Whoa...them stars are pretty..." he said drunkenly.

When Maggie reached the mud, she slowly waddled into the sticky goopy substance. She looked back at the gaggle of ducks who were waving her on. With a sigh, she began to roll in the mud.

"That's it!" yelled Duke, "more! More!"

Maggie dove in now, splashing, rolling and tossing mud everywhere. She was so covered with mud that her orange eyes were the only things visible.

"I think he's comin'!" yelled Duke, "Keep it up!"

Maggie tossed mud everywhere and found herself enjoying it. She chuckled as she flung mud into the air and felt it splatter onto her back and wings.

"He's comin' down!" yelled Streak.

Maggie was so excited. Finally, there was something she was good at. Finally, she felt a part of something. "They NEED me," she thought.

"They LIKE me."

Then Maggie began to hear a sound. It wasn't the sound she expected to hear, not the flapping of wings, or the distant cry of the Mud Hawk. It was more like "AACK, aack, aack, aack!" It wasn't very loud, but it became a sound she knew well. A sound she'd heard all her life.

It was the sound of laughter.

The ducks were laughing so hard some of them are tipping over in the water, or holding their feathery chests with one wing and slapping the water with the other.

"Don't that beat all!" squawked Streak, barely able to speak.

"A Mud Duck!" honked Rufus, "Now I done seen ever'thang!"

Duke pointed to Maggie, who was covered in mud and standing perfectly still.

"Look at that, boys!" he cackled, "I never suspected anythin' could make her look more homelier than she was before, but gol' danged if we ain't done it!"

"Hey Miss Mud Duck, Ma'am!" called one of the ducks, "why don't you jes' keep rollin' around 'n maybe the Mud Hawk'll come down and give you a big kiss!" They all busted up with laughter.

Maggie put her head down and slowly walked into the water.

"What's all over that gol' darn duck?" some duck asked. "Did she fall in the mud?"

"That's not a duck," replied another, "she's a pig!"

"A Mud Cluck!"

"I think she looks better this way!"

"Oink, oink, oink!"

Maggie swam away from the hysterical ducks, her head very low, almost touching the water.

"Hey! Better wash all that off, darlin'! Ya' get out in the sun an' it'll dry up. Then you might 'quack'."

They roared with laughter again as Maggie gained distance. As the sun set, she still heard their laughter, even halfway across the pond.

Maggie slapped the water and made her memory disappear in the ripples of the pond. Her eyes narrowed and her jaw set, fighting back the tears.

"If I could," she thought, "I'd change 'em all into the ugliest things in the world!" She looked in the water again, a vision appeared of the gang ducks laughing at her. Then they began to change, mutate, their bodies twisting, crying out for help. Ripples washed the vision away.

CHAPTER THREE

Not far away, just onshore, two moles were sitting before a small fire tossing in sticks and rubbing their hands together with eagerness. On a rock, between the fire and the water, sat a green frog. It was not just any green frog that sat upon the rock. This frog was dressed in formal black tails, with a red sash draped smartly over one shoulder, and a monocle placed like a jewel over his right eye. His name was Sir Archibald Rivvitt the third. Sir Archibald stood on the rock, cleared his puffy throat, and began speaking to the two moles, who gave him every bit of the small attention they possessed.

"So it must be stolen in the morning. There will be no guards posted at the palace. They'll all be busy with morning drills. The King, of course, will be out for his morning swim."

One of the moles, named Charlie, raised a hand.

"Yes, yes…" said the frog impatiently, "what is it?"

Charlie spoke in a nasally Brooklyn accent.

"Dat's great, but we can't swim. How we gonna get the necklace off this guy if he's swimmin'?"

"Yeah, dat would be a predicament boy, lemme tell ya'," said the other mole, named Irving.

"He's not going to be wearing the necklace, you brainless sot!" The frog glowered at the moles through his monocle making his frog eye seem enormous.

"Oooh! Dat's weird!" Charlie whispered.

"He NEVER swims with the necklace on," Archibald continued. "The idiot says it slows down his 'racing speed'. Whatever that is..." He puffed up his chest. "Why, I could outswim him with both feet tied behind my back."

"I don't get it," Irving said, poking the fire. "If we steal it, and you come back with it, they're gonna know you took it. You ain't no good ta' us in jail."

"Yeah, boy…" Charlie said, still staring at the frog's monocle.

"Shift the blame gentlemen!" said Archibald. "Merely shift the blame. I've been doing it all my life to great success. After I'm done with my cousin, they'll believe he's in league with Toad himself! Pompous old fools! They actually believe there IS a Toad. It's all poppycock and legend, years old, but they'll still believe me. Especially when I bring witnesses...."

"Okay, but what about the necklace?" Irving went on, scratching his head. "YOU said you needed the necklace cause it was magic. YOU said you could use the magic of the necklace ta' change us. YOU said--"

"I KNOW WHAT I SAID!" the frog bellowed. The moles jumped back, startled. Archibald composed himself and smoothed out the wrinkles in his coat.

"The magic of the necklace is real, of course, but that's history--What's really important here is BREEDING!"

Charlie and Irving were completely lost, which was not new. Their teeny tiny brains could only hold so much information, and they'd been working overtime. Archibald knew the moles were thin in the thoughts department. That's why he had chosen them. Archibald Rivvit the third was extremely clever, and as most clever creatures know, stupidity is one of the few things in the world that can truly be trusted.

"Let me explain," he said, "in child-like terms." He spread his chubby arms wide. His face became a mixture of green from his frog skin, and the orange light from the flames.

"In the beginning there was mud. And mud was all there was...then, lightning struck the mud, and mountains, seas, ponds and rivers sprang into being. Lightning struck again, and out of the mud came life! Trees, grass, lilies,...life without intelligence. But when lightning struck a third time, it left behind something incredible! A creature of great intelligence. Magnificent beauty. Stunning regality! Yes, gentlemen, yes! A FROG! And this creature, the Great Frog, knew the power of the mud and called it "Rivvit." And it was good...." Archibald stopped, his chest heaving. His big round yellow eyes gazed into the fire, lost in the ancient past.

"Still, the Great Frog soon grew bored. But...the Great Frog knew the power of the mud and what he must do. So he sat in the mud, and power flowed through him. He raised his arm and it became lightning itself. He began to change the simple life around him into other things, more complex creatures, creatures that flew, walked and swam.

And again he saw it was good.

But, the Great Frog was still lonely. So he sat in the mud again, and THIS time he made frogs! And by Jove, gentlemen, it was more than good, it was brilliant!" Archibald laughed a victorious laugh and seemed to dance on the rock, until he almost fell back into the water. He composed himself and began again.

"In time, the mud of power began to dry. Before it was gone, the Great Frog took some of the mud in his hands and fashioned a medallion on a necklace of silver. A medallion that has been in the Rivvit family since the beginning of time. No King of Royal Pond has ever ruled without it, and I am not about to be the first!"

Charlie and Irving sat silently, with their mouths hanging open.

"Wow...great story," Charlie said reverently, "now....tell me dat part again about life without intelligence..."

Archibald rolled his eyes and pressed his hands against the sides of his head until his eyes bulged.

Irving had been playing with a twig, poking it in the fire. He pointed the glowing tip at Archibald.

"So you're sure it works, right? You can use it ta' turn us into humans like we want?"

"Precisely," Archibald nodded, amazed that one or two of his words had actually reached their itsy bitsy minds. Irving was squinting, trying hard to figure out all the angles.

"But what's ta' stop us from just usin' this necklace ourselves?" he said.

"Why, what an intelligent question," Archibald said. "I'm shocked."

"Brains an' good looks, dat's me, boy!" Irving said beaming.

The frog puffed up again and hopped closer to the two moles. He leaned in and pulled his lower eyelid down, exposing a big yellow bloodshot eye.

"Do you notice the color of my eyes?"

"Oooh," Charlie said, "weird..."

"Yeah..." Irving added, "you ought'tah get more sleep."

"My eyes are YELLOW, is the point! Only those frogs of the royal line, those who have the blood of the Great Frog in their veins, have yellow eyes."

"Spooky....." Charlie whispered.

"Sooooo....the two of you don't have yellow eyes, do you?"

The moles shook their heads like Siamese twins.

"So if you tried to use it, it would change whoever you used it ON into something more hideous than you could possibly imagine!!"

Just then, a "ROAR" came from the distance. Irving immediately started clawing his way up on Charlie's back. They were both shivering violently. Irving kept trying to climb higher and higher on Charlie's back using the hair on Charlie's head. Charlie's face looked like Chinese dragon.

The sound passed and they relaxed.

Archibald noticed this fear of bears and placed it in the vast library of cunning thoughts he carried around in his mind. He had learned that cunning thoughts were good to have around. Like an extra pair of socks, one never knew when one might need them.

Irving still had his twig with the smoking red-hot tip in his hand. As he slid down Charlie's back, he kept one arm around Charlie's throat, but the other arm with the glowing twig jammed into Charlie's furry behind. Charlie and Irving began to sniff the air.

"What the...hey, dat's a funny smell..." Charlie said.

"Yeah. Sort o' smells like..."

With a "POOF", Charlie's bottom burst into fire.

"AHHH!" Charlie screamed and ran in twisted circles as flames trailed behind him. Irving was bouncing up and down on his back like he was riding a bucking bronco. Charlie made a sharp turn, which sent Irving flying, as Charlie dashed for the water. Charlie jumped in and heard a comforting "HISS" as the fire went out.

Irving dusted himself off and absently tossed his twig into the fire. The fire and anything bright hypnotized him.

"Ya' see", he said, in a trance, "we're almost human. We can make fire. Geeze..."

"Yeah, see?" Charlie said pointing to the fire with chattering teeth and dripping with water.

"Yes, I see." Archibald responded with a sneer, "I feel so secure knowing the two of you have the knowledge to burn down the whole forest."

Irving pulled out a shiny piece of glass from his shorts. They liked to wear whatever human things they could find. Even though sometimes they didn't know how to wear it. They were often seen by the various animals in the forest, wearing human underwear over their heads.

Holding up the glass, he said, "Charlie and me found this when we were diggin'."

Charlie wasn't paying attention. Archibald's monocle was shining in the firelight. Charlie was drawn to it as if it were a magnet.

"You got a nice glass shiny too..." he said, hypnotized by the shiny monocle. He was poking his finger closer and closer to Archibald's eye. Archibald swatted the hand away.

"Get away from me, you peasant!"

Irving knocked Charlie out of the way and held out his own piece of glass for Archibald to see.

"This one makes things hot when ya' hold it in the sun. The moon don't do anything to it though. We tried." He held it up and looked at the moon through it. Charlie reached over and grabbed it away from him.

"My turn to hold it!" he said.

"Is not!" said Irving.

"Is so!"

Charlie and Irving scuffled, rolling around on the ground, muttering statements like, "give it back, you lousy skunk breath," or "it's my turn, worm brain."

Archibald held his hands up to the sky in despair. He walked to the two moles wrestling on the ground, leaned down and calmly said, "Oh my! What shall I do! Oh dear me! A bear! A nasty old bear!"

The moles froze.

"He's comin' for us!" Charlie whispered.

"Ahh! We're gonna die!" Irving cried.

"I'm too young!"

"Too handsome!!!"

"I'm in my prime!"

Archibald waddled a few feet in front of them, hands on his hips.

"Now, I realize how amazingly short your attention spans are, so I will make this brief---- Tomorrow morning you will steal the necklace..."

The two moles never moved.

"...you will then take it downstream to the wash, where you will await my arrival..." Archibald strutted to the edge of the rock and gestured in grand fashion. "Then, I shall approach the great Council and proclaim in a loud voice: "My Lords! The King, my Cousin, is a liar, a thief, and a traitor!" Archibald's eyes became teary, and he proceeded in a quaking voice.

"Oh what a woeful day! What a burden I bear, my Lords. My own cousin...a common criminal!" Archibald began playing to an imaginary audience.

"What? I, my Lords? Yes, it is true that I'm the only male heir, but, I'm far too humble a frog to be 'King'. A simple frog, a kind frog, a frog content merely to serve in humility. A frog that--"

"What a fathead," Charlie whispered to Irving.

"Maybe that's how they float so good," Irving replied. "Big bug eyes too..."

"Wish we had some popcorn--"

"Shut up!!" Archibald shouted, whirling on the two moles. "I was practicing my speech, and now you've ruined it. Blast!" He pointed a webbed finger at them. "Listen you two...after one full moon, with or without the necklace, I shall be crowned King! When I appear at the coronation WITH the necklace, my destiny will be fulfilled. Then, and only then will I turn you into humans. IS THAT CLEAR! Though, why you don't want to be something more 'evolved' I'll never know. And by the way," he said, hopping over so close to Charlie and Irving the two moles leaned backwards. "If you bungle this...I'll use the necklace on you anyway. But I won't turn you into humans. I'll turn the both of you into fish food!"

Archibald hopped to the rock, into the water, glared at them, turned, dove into the water, and swam away.

"Wow, dat guy's intense," Charlie said.

"Dat's for sure," replied Irving and suddenly swatted something black that flew straight at his face.

Suddenly, three black shapes darted in and out of the light, in and out of the flames, doing aerobatics and laughing . They cruised around Charlie and Irving's heads as the moles tried desperately to swat them away.

Laughing at the mole's feeble attempts, the three bats landed on the rock, grinning with their pointy teeth. Their eyes glowed orange in the firelight. The bats, Miguel, Pilar, and Hector crossed their arms and smiled at the moles.

"Hey, Hermanos! Long time no see, man," Hector said.

"Your friend's pretty uptight for a green guy, eh?" asked Miguel.

"Yeah," Hector added, "like maybe he got chu' all scared now and you forgot about your deal with our boss?"

"That'd be too bad, chu' know," said Pilar, sharpening her claws on the rock. "Cause our boss, he wouldn't like it, chu' know, if you backed out on your deal."

"Yeah," Miguel said, "Then he might have to get ugly. More ugly than he already is heh, heh, heh...."

"Hey!" Hector said in a whisper, slapping Miguel with his wing, "'chut' up, man! What's wrong wit' choo'?"

Miguel suddenly looked worried.

"What? Ju' think somebody heard me, or sometheen'?"

"Look, you two furballs," cut in Pilar, pointing her wing at the moles, "You give us the necklace, like you promised. Then our boss likes you, ju' know. Then you get like, "protection" see?"

"Yeah," said Irving, narrowing his eyes and looking sideways at Charlie, "but, we don't get dis' protection part. Ya' know? I mean, protection from what?"

"Yeah, protection from what?" Charlie repeated.

"Our boss, he's got lots o' friends that owe him, like, favors, ju' know? Like, he's got this one friend, that's big and hairy and brown...with all these teeth, and likes to eat little molie dudes like you."

With perfect timing, a roar echoed in the distance. The two moles scurried down to the water, putting the fire between them and the noise. Charlie was wild-eyed and biting his nails.

"You mean your boss knows 'dat bear?"

Pilar flitted onto the ground in front of the moles.

"The boss knows everybody. And you two molie boys better not pull no double cross, if you know what's good for ju'. You don't get that necklace for him and there's no hole deep enough for you to hide. You get me?"

Miguel snickered as the smoke from the fire wafted over him.

"Hey, hee, hee, can you just see the boss crawlin' down a hole, man, with his big ole' fat belly and-"

Hector slapped a wing over Miguel's mouth.

"Would ju' chut up, man! You got this self-destructive side to you, don't chu'? Ju' know the boss got spies everywhere, man!"

Miguel's eyes went a little cross-eyed and he teetered from side to side. He was trying to fan away the smoke.

"Whew, I feel dizzy, Ese'. Must be the smoke."

Pilar, fed up with her companions, took to the air. Hector didn't realize the meeting was over.

"Hey, where you going, woman?"

"Away from ju', ju' big dope."

Hector and Miguel took off as well, toward the moon. As they fluttered away, Hector and Miguel continued their conversation.

"Maybe you're like... in a dream-state, ju' know?

With the smoke and the fire and everytheen'. A Castaneda theen'."

"I don't know, man. Like, was he dizzy too?"

"Yeah, but on purpose, I think."

"Would ju' two chut' up!" shouted Pilar. "Your driveen' me crazy. You're so stupid ju' don't know!"

Miguel flapped up in the air along side Pilar and, in a flirting way, bumped into her.

"Ooooh I'm so scared." he said.

"You should be.....and don't touch me... one wing-span apart. I tol' ju' before!

"My wings are so long, I'd have ta' be next ta' that moon so's not to touch you, baby..."

"In your dreams. You rodent!" Pilar sped up ahead of them.

"I know you are, but what am I?" Hector called to her. Miguel trailed behind, flying crookedly and trying to keep up.

"Hey you guys...I think I'm gonna hurl, man..."

Someone hidden in the reeds, Maggie was still watching the moles. She was thinking hard. She'd been curious about the fire and swam through the reeds close enough to hear the conversation between Archibald and the moles. The bats as well. But it was Archibald's words that kept echoing in her mind:

"It would turn them into something more hideous than you could possibly imagine..."

CHAPTER FOUR

Outside the Frog Palace that same night, trumpets were blaring and thousands of frog voices were crying out: "Hail Theodore! Long live the King! Hail Theodore! Long live the King!"

The joyous voices slowly faded as everyone watched the moon rise over the great hill. This was part of the Ceremony of the Full Moon, a frog ceremony that took place once each month. The moon rose to the sound of an orchestra of pond musicians. Bullfrogs were tubas, mosquitoes were the flutes, crickets were violins. Their music stands were lit by fireflies, and fireflies lit up the palace grounds as well.

The music grew as the moon finally cleared the mountain peak and the conductor of the orchestra gave an energetic cutoff to the musicians. He swung his baton so excitedly, it knocked him off his feet and he went crashing into the cricket section.

Inside the Palace, within the Royal Quarters, a skinny frog named, Richfield, with droopy eyelids, and a red bow tie, was arranging the clothing of another frog standing before him. The frog being dressed had a very frustrated look on his face.

"Blast! Blast! Blast! Double blast! I don't see

how my showing up for these functions is necessary. It's so blasted stupid!" Richfield didn't bother to look up, as he spoke.

"But your highness, the waterbug races are about to start. And tomorrow night is the full moon. And the ball. And you are the King. The clothes I've picked out for tonight will be a smash at the ball."

"Who cares about the ruddy ball! I want to have fun." Richfield said nothing, but adjusted the King's tie.

"And every full moon it's always the same!"

"But it's the King's duty."

"I never asked to be King! Did I? Is it my fault if I was born "better" than everyone else? Gad, no! I tell you, Richfield, you simply don't know what a bother the poor and lowly can be!"

Richfield held up a beautiful green and silver necklace.

"And this necklace, that's another thing. Thank goodness I can take it off while I swim. It's heavy. And it chafes. YOU try sleeping with it on."

Richfield held out the necklace and Theodore walked forward, poking his wide frog head into it.

"Let someone else preside at these ridiculous functions. Someone who enjoys them...let my cousin Archie do it."

"But your Highness, your cousin, the Duke, is

not King. You are. Listen to them cry out for you! They want King Theodore. And it's only right and fitting that they should have him." Richfield stepped back and appraised his work.

"There now..."

Theodore moved over to a long mirror and viewed himself. He assumed a regal pose. Then he began to make faces, royal faces. Richfield folded his hands.

"You look divine, your Highness."

"Oh that's what you always say, Richfield. Just once I'd like to hear you say "You look horrible" or "What a fright you are today." Richfield held out a long red robe and Theodore stepped into it.

"Speaking of 'fright', Richfield, you haven't seen my cousin Archie about have you?"

"Why no, your Highness.

"I don't like it when I don't know where he is. It's well known cousin Archie doesn't love me... Why even as polliwogs he'd pull my tail, or push me onto dry land....always hated that."

"Jealousy Your Highness. He resents your being King and wearing the Royal Necklace."

"Well, let HIM deal with peasants all day then. See how HE likes it! Peasants are always wanting things. I don't need anything, why should they? I mean, I'm incredibly rich and they're desperately poor...but, peasants are SUPPOSED to be poor, aren't they? I mean, that's why they're peasants, hang it all."

Theodore looked down at his right hand. "Richfield, you haven't seen my ring about have you?"

"No, Your Highness."

"Don't know where the silly thing could be."

"Your Highness should mount the throne now so that the Nobles can present themselves." Richfield swung open some tall doors made of reeds.

"The "Nobles," old prune faces! Richfield, perhaps we could skip the ceremony, eh? Just this once, eh, Richfield?"

"I am but a lowly servant your Highness."

"Oh stop it! I hate it when you do that."

CHAPTER FIVE

In the morning, beside a stream that eventually fed into the pond, there stood a tall oak. Tufts of grass grew around the tree and up the mossy bank like green syrup. To one side of the tree, a colony of mice went about their daily routines. Jeremy, and Alice sat on adjoining acorns under the tree, watching everyone and arguing.

"...I just don't see why?" Jeremy asked for the fourteenth time, "I have a little cottage...a good business?"

"You're a TAILOR, Jeremy! I mean, how exciting is that?"

"Well, it's dangerous work, I mean...there are needles all over the place!"

Alice got up off her acorn and walked around primping up her hair. "I want someone dashing. Someone who'll sweep me off my feet."

"I could do that! I could start doing pushups..."

"It's not just that I want someone brave, adventurous."

"Well, I'm working on this new piece with a plunging neckline and--"

While Jeremy was explaining how he could fit Alice's "husband" requirements, Alice was watching another mouse some distance away, climb a small seedling. She happened to catch the eye of the mouse. He stopped and waved. She gave a flirting little wave back.

Jeremy went into an incredible panic. "There's just nothing to be brave about, Alice! Not here!"

As if on cue, at that moment, horns of alarm sounded. Two large furry creatures with sharp little teeth came running through the colony causing screams and cries of panic. They were the moles, Charlie and Irving, who were not terribly huge, but to mice, everything is huge. Charlie had a silver chain hanging out of his mouth which he kept dropping, or getting tangled around his foot. The mice scattered in all directions, running for their lives.

Jeremy froze in terror. His tail went rigid and quivering.

Alice happened to be directly in the moles' path. She screamed for Jeremy, but Jeremy was too frightened to move. In a flash, the mouse who had been climbing the seedling, dropped to the ground and grabbed his bow. He bounded over to Alice and stood in front of her, right in the path of the oncoming moles. From his bow, he shot a tiny arrow which landed in Charlie's rear leg. The Charlie let out a shriek of pain and his hair stood out all over his body like a porcupine. Irving ran back, grabbed him, and dragged him away.

As the two moles disappeared into the woods, the mice came out of hiding. Jeremy slowly unfroze. He was terribly embarrassed, but tried not to show it as he came over to check on Alice.

"Boy, that was a close one," he said.

Alice made no attempt to hide her disgust.

"I could have been killed! If it hadn't been for this...this...very brave, handsome mouse, I wouldn't even BE here now! And what were YOU doing?

You were scared stiff! There's no way I'm going to marry you! You...you...coward!"

"Well, they were bigger than me!" Jeremy pleaded.

The other mouse, Alice's rescuer, was still standing next to her. She turned to him.

"Would you walk me home? This has all been too much for me. I feel a little weak."

The other mouse put an arm around Alice's shoulder and they walked away. Alice was in full flirting mode. It was her best mode, even though it didn't last very long after she got what she wanted.

"I'm so weak, I wouldn't be surprised if you had to carry me."

"Alice!" Jeremy called after her, "Wait! Please! I can be brave! Just give me a chance!" But Alice never looked back.

Dejected, and thoroughly depressed, Jeremy walked back to his shop.

Jeremy entered his tailor shop and put on his apron as he stared into space. An older mouse, Jonathan, was over by the window sewing. Jeremy took off the apron he had just put on and threw it to the ground.

"Something on your mind?" asked Jonathan absently.

"I'm going to have to leave, Jonathan."

"Really? That so?"

"I can't do things here! There's no adventure here! Don't you understand! I HAVE to have some adventure in my life! I just HAVE to!"

Jonathan never looked up from the vest he was sewing.

"Does that, Alice, girl have anything to do with this?"

"Hah! Alice? Don't be ridiculous! I'm through with her! She was boring. I need adventure. You know me. I need excitement all the time! Yes sir! You don't expect me to be a tailor all my life do you?"

Jonathan finally looked up at Jeremy, peering over his spectacles.

"Oh...sorry, Jonathan. I didn't mean it that way." He took a determined breath. "But, I've just got to seek my fortune. Find out what I want in life. You know? Then I can come back, and be a tailor, and, and ...well, whatever."

"Boy, I've known you all your life, and I can tell which thoughts started out in your own head, and which thoughts got 'put' there. And being that there's so much empty room in your head, it leaves a lot of space for others to put things in it."

"Jonathan, you're not helping."

"Look, boy, either somebody loves you, or they don't. That's all there is to it. You can't run your life tryin' to be what somebody wants you to be. And young Miss Alice, I'm afraid, will never be through wantin' things she doesn't have, and complainin' about the things she does."

"No," Jeremy said, shaking his head, "no, Alice is right. I'm just a coward." Jeremy paced back and forth. Jonathan watched him.

"I've made up my mind, Jonathan. I've got to go and seek my fortune. That's it. No other way around it." Jonathan went back to sewing.

"Of course, you can have the business until I get back. If I get back. You were my father's closest friend, Jonathan. And mine, too." Jonathan kept sewing. Jeremy kept waiting...and waiting for Jonathan to try to talk him out of it. "Well, aren't you going to say anything!"

Finally Jonathan looked up.

"A mouse has to do what a mouse has to do." He said and put the work down. "And maybe you're right. Maybe this is something you have to do." Jonathan left his bench and walked over to a tiny window in the corner. "But, you'll take care of yourself, won't you, laddie?"

Jeremy realized this was as emotional as Jonathan would allow himself to be.

"Course," Jeremy said.

Jonathan sniffed and pulled himself together. "We best get you packed then. No time like the present."

"Thanks, old friend," said Jeremy, smiling. Jonathan nodded and they both looked out the window. It was the easiest way not to look at each other.

CHAPTER SIX

At Festival Cove, a part of the pond shadowed by an overhanging cliff, hundreds of frogs were gathered on carpets of lilies, cheering and hopping in and out of the water.

On shore, sitting on a large rock covered in moss, sat Theodore. Two bullfrogs, Palace Guards, stood puffed up on either side of him. The orchestra was playing a waltz which seemed to go perfectly with the approach of an old fat frog who could barely hop from one lily pad to the next. Each time he hopped you could hear him grunting. He was loaded with medals and decorations which, surely, would pull him straight to the bottom should he ever actually fall in the water. Following him, was a more slender frog who easily bounced from one leaf to another. With a final loud grunt, both landed on a lily pad in front of Theodore.

The orchestra leader made a massive cut-off and fell crashing into the beetle percussion section.

The Court Crier, a frog dressed all in red with a white wig, stood up on a log that was wedged in the mud and called to those on shore:

"Lords and Ladies...the Prime Minister, Lord Hopkins and Minister of Justice, Baron Von Puddle."

Baron Von Puddle, the Minister of Justice, stood

in the rear with his feet folded behind his back. Lord Hopkins, the Prime Minister, puffed up his throat and rattled his many medals as he spoke through his two buck teeth.

"Your Majesty," said Lord Hopkins, bowing, "Salutations on this the second day of the full moon. Your people send their praises. Yes, they do." He bowed again. "Today we have the jumping contests, the races, and, oh, of course, the Grand Ball this evening, and...and...your Highness? Your Highness is not wearing the Royal Necklace."

Theodore looked down sheepishly.

"Did you forget to wear it, sire?"

Theodore was silent.

"Shall I send the guards to fetch it?"

Theodore looked at Lord Hopkins with big yellow eyes and swallowed hard.

"I can't find it," Theodore mumbled.

"Hmmm? What did you say, your Highness?" Hopkins asked, leaning closer.

"I can't find it," Theodore mumbled again.

"What?" Hopkins asked, cupping one ear.

"I CAN'T FIND IT!!" Theodore finally yelled out loud.

The Prime Minister's jaw dropped and his hand went for his heart. Whispers spread throughout the crowd like rustling grass.

"Surely you can't mean that you've lost it, your

Majesty!!"

"No! No, No I didn't say that...I merely said that I can't FIND it."

"Why, this is unheard of, your Majesty! How could you possibly not be able to "find" the Royal Necklace!"

"Well, I got back from my swim this morning and it was gone. I had it last night. It must have been misplaced or...something…"

"Or something!" Hopkins yelled. "Or something! The Royal Necklace misplaced!" This caused everyone in the court and all those on the lilies of the Pond grew silent.

"It's not my fault!" Theodore whined. "I always put it on my dressing table before my swim. But this morning when I returned, it was gone."

Lord Hopkins was beside himself.

"But...But...But...This is impossible! Misplaced! Gone? Guards! Guards!"

Frog guards came streaming in from all directions, surrounding Lord Hopkins, Baron Von Puddle, and Theodore.

"Go to the King's chambers at once! Search everywhere! The Royal Necklace must be found!"

The guards hopped away in two lines and Lord Hopkins glared at Theodore, so agitated his eyes were rolling around in circles.

"I'm sure we'll find it, Hopkins," said Theodore,

trying to regain his kingly manner. "After all it's just an old necklace."

"You fool!" Hopkins hissed.

Theodore was taken aback that anyone could speak to him that way. Lord Hopkins shocked himself, too. He lowered his voice so as not to alarm the already astounded crowd.

"Do you realize what you've done! That necklace has tremendous importance! It is the foundation of our empire!"

"Well....it's not my fault!" Theodore said, throwing a little tantrum. "How am I supposed to keep track of the silly thing!"

The rest of the Lords of the Council gathered around Lord Hopkins and Baron Von Puddle. They all looked extremely grave.

The frog in the white wig entered the circle of Lords, clasped his hands together and raised his chin. He puffed up and announced to the crowd:

"Lords and ladies…Sir Archibald Rivvit, Lord of Moss, Duke of Lily."

Archibald, strode through the crowd. He marched up before the Lords and made a token bow to them as a group. He seemed very agitated which made his cheeks more red than green.

"My Lords!" Archibald began, "Oh, my Lords! I am filled today with grief and shock! It's too much for one frog to bear, I tell you! Simply too much!"

"What is the meaning of this, Lord Rivvit?" Baron Von Puddle said. "We have an emergency. We don't have time--"

"Emergency, yes, my Lords!" Archibald interrupted. "It is precisely this emergency which has brought me here so late." Archie faced Theodore.

"My Lords, the King, my cousin, my.... Monarch, sadly, is a liar, a womanizer, and a TRAITOR!" Archibald pointed a finger at Theodore and turned his head as if in disgrace. "He has had the necklace, the Royal Necklace, stolen, and intends to run away and use it for his own selfish ends!"

"This is preposterous!" said Von Puddle. "My dear Duke, this can't be true!"

Theodore's eyes were like two big moons now. The other members of Court, teetered forward to bend an ear. The Ladies of the Court were fluttering their handkerchiefs, about to pass out. Some fainted straight away. Another frog, stepped forward, limping. His name was Lord Brimbly.

"Explain yourself, Lord Rivvit! These are serious charges."

"No more serious than what has already happened because of my cousin! The necklace has not been stolen, my Lords. No. It has been SOLD! Even as we speak, the agents of the King are making their way across the "Hills of the Sun" to the "Great River!" in order to deliver the necklace!"

Theodore finally spoke up. "Deliver the necklace? Preposterous! Why in heaven's name would I do that?"

Archibald still refused to look at Theodore. He halted the King's speech with closed eyes and an upraised hand.

"My Lords, the tale becomes far worse, I'm afraid."

"But why would he do such a thing?" asked Lord Hopkins. "And deliver it to whom?"

Archibald gulped dramatically, as if he dare not say the next word.

"Toad," he said softly. The name came out like a curse.

Theodore was in shock.

Military guards, dressed in different colors than those worn by the palace guards, entered, flanking a voluptuous female frog with big red lips and great gobs of blue eye shadow. The female frog, "Gypsy" by name, strutted up to the now catatonic Theodore, and gave him a huge kiss on the cheek. The kiss left behind enormous red lip marks on Theodore's cheek.

"This is the woman," Archibald began, "my cousin has been seeing for months. He revealed everything to her of his plan! And how, in exchange for the necklace, Toad would make him ruler of not only Royal Pond, but all Waterlands beyond!"

"But who is this woman?" asked Lord Brimbly. "Is she of noble blood?"

"No, my Lord," said Archibald. "Her name is Gypsy, it seems. And she is a uh....well, a cabaret singer."

Several Lords dropped their monocles to the floor.

"A what!" said Lord Hopkins, aghast. "A-a-a-a-a-cabaret singer! You mean..."

Another Lord, Lord Flipton, walked forward. He had huge feet and a monstrous pot belly that bounced on the ground as he walked. He pointed a finger at Gypsy.

"Young woman?"

Gypsy replied in a thick cockney accent.

"You talkin' to me, Dearie?"

Lord Flipton cleared his throat.

"Young woman, what have you to say for yourself?"

Gypsy turned to the assembly and pulled out a handkerchief. She was a very bad actress, but well rehearsed.

"Well, Teddy 'n me..." she began, and the Lords leaned back, visibly shaken by the fact that she called the King, 'Teddy', "...we met each day during his swim. He said it was the only place he wouldn't

42

be followed and that no one would find us."

Theodore's mouth dropped to the floor.

"We was in love, we was. But, he said it wouldn't work. He said no one would let the King marry a poor 'umble girl like me. Just an innocent girl without any noble blood." She paused a moment to blow her nose. "I cried my eyes out, I did. So, he told me of his plan with this 'Toad' person, whoever he is."

She looked earnestly at the Lords, who now had changed their expressions to that of sympathy.

"I said, "No! You mustn't do that Teddy! You mustn't up and give the Royal Necklace to nobody! The Royal Necklace, is what our 'ole society, our entire socio-economic system is based on, not to mention the cultural effect of myth on the populace! It's just not--"

"Gad!" Archibald said through tight lips, "Get on with it, woman!"

"Well," Gypsy continued, "he said not to worry and that he was a genius, and that after Toad worked things out, he wouldn't just have power over Royal Pond no more, but over all the wetlands in Toad's kingdom. Well, I was embarrassed and became quite flushed as I'm known to do." She turned to Theodore and tickled under his chin.

Lord Hopkins was clutching his heart.

"My Lords! Toad! Toad is alive!!!"

"That's impossible!" Lord Flipton screeched. "He was banished from Royal Pond generations ago!"

Lord Hopkins looked very weary. His droopy eyes were wide with terror.

"Nothing was ever a greater threat to the Pond than Toad."

Gypsy scrunched up Theodore's face with her hands and looked him soulfully. "I'm sorry me' darlin'."

Theodore was stunned senseless. Lord Hopkins stomped over to Theodore, his fluffy brows hanging over his eyes.

"Well? Have you anything to say for yourself?"

Theodore snapped out of his stupor.

"It's a lie, of course! It's all a lie! I've never met this woman in my life!"

"Uh...well...he did give me this, your Lordship," said Gypsy, holding out a hand upon which rested a ruby ring.

"The Rivvit Family ring!" Lord Flipton gasped.

Theodore blinked in astonishment. One of the guards caught him as he began to faint.

Archibald examined the hand.

"Richfield! Come here! Is this the King's ring?"

Richfield suddenly appeared from out of the crowd. He walked up to Gypsy and took her hand, examining the ring. He looked up at Gypsy.

"In need of a manicure, are we?"

"Just look at the ring, you fool!" Archibald barked.

"Yes, this is the ring," Richfield said. "The Rivvit Family ring."

"Has the King been acting...suspiciously of late?"

Richfield looked at Theodore sheepishly.

"Well, his swims have been longer than normal, as I recall. And upon several occasions, I've noticed seeing reddish imprints upon his face. A bit like...that"

Richfield pointed to the lip marks on Theodore's face. Theodore looked up in horror.

"Richfield! You too?"

"That will be all, Richfield," Archibald ordered.

Richfield backed away, and the Lords tightened their circle around Theodore. Lord Hopkins shoved his face up against Theodore's.

"Your Highness. It would be best if you would return to your chambers. The Palace Guard will accompany you to keep you...safe."

"But it's not true!" Theodore pleaded. "None of this is true!" The guards lifted Theodore up by the arms and escorted him out.

"Wait! Please! They're lying!" Theodore continued to shout as the guards dragged him back into the palace, as he struggled, but slid smoothly atop his long red kingly robe.

CHAPTER SEVEN

At dawn the next morning Theodore was lying in a pile of crumpled sheets on his bed. He'd had a wrestling match with them during the night. The sheets were snakes wrapping their coils around him, while Archibald was sitting on the Theodore's throne egging the snakes on.

He awoke when the door swung open and guards marched into the room. They roused him from his sleep and, still wearing the clothes from the day before, escorted him outside.

As Theodore's eyes grew accustomed to the bright morning light, he began to make out the shapes of thousands of frogs seated on lilies across the whole pond. They also lined the shores as far as he could see. The Lords were all lined up, waiting for him. Lord Hopkins was the first to speak.

"Theodore Rivvit, you have been found guilty of high treason for aiding a villain whose very name brings fear. Toad. An enemy of all those on Royal Pond. You are also found guilty of seeking your own material gain over that of the subjects who serve and rely upon you." Theodore looked beaten and pitiful. Lord Hopkins continued.

"It is a sad duty we have, but a duty that is clear. Ordinarily, anyone found guilty of high treason would be tied to stakes and placed in the hot sun. But you are of royal blood, and those of royal blood cannot be put to death."

Through the throng of frogs, Jeremy, the mouse, made his way, a knapsack tied onto a pole that was slung over one shoulder. Few frogs noticed him except to stare and to move aside. Jeremy stopped when he was far enough forward to peer over some of the green heads. Lord Flipton began to pace in front of Theodore.

"We are faced with two choices then: to imprison you, or banish you. For this decision we must turn to the one next in line by blood to take the throne."

Archibald strutted forward pompously. He raised his hand in the air.

"If we should imprison him, what is to stop him from still plotting insurrection by means of his many spies? What is to stop him from passing secrets onto Toad? No, no my lords, banishment is the only judgment that can be made."

Lord Hopkins sighed.

"Very well. So be it."

The guards took Theodore forward past the edge of the mud to the crest of the pond bank. The brightly dressed court crier walked in front of the vast gathering and pulled out a scroll. He began to read in a loud voice.

"Henceforth, let it be known that King Theodore of Rivvit the fifth is hereby and forever banished from Royal Pond. Anyone aiding him will be banished as well. His name shall be stricken from all Royal Pond history. His crown is hereby revoked. This decree shall be signed by the new King who will be crowned at the next full moon,

Archibald Rivvit III." The Crier folded up his scroll.

Archibald was smiling smugly.

Theodore had a big tear rolling down one cheek. He pleaded with the crowd before him.

"Won't anyone believe me!! I'm innocent!!"

The crowd did not respond. They didn't have to. He was no longer their king.

"Very well! I will find the real thieves and bring them back! Rest assured!!" He took a deep breath and puffed up. "Is there no one brave enough to accompany me? Someone who is fearless enough to be my champion?"

No one stepped forward.

Theodore deflated until his fingertips touched the ground. Then, from the amidst of the crowd, he heard a small voice.

"Uh, right here!" Jeremy called, holding up a finger. "I will, Sire!"

Theodore looked up to see a small field mouse with a knapsack over one shoulder step out from the crowd. The whispering this caused among the frogs sounded like wind through trees. Jeremy walked up to Theodore and knelt on one knee before him.

"I'll go with you, Sire. I'll be your champion," he said.

Theodore shook off his stunned look and reassumed his normal superior attitude. He spoke more to the crowd than to the mouse.

"Very well then, good mouse, being the bravest here, I give you the privilege of accompanying me. And as for all of you..." he said, pointing at

Archibald and the Lords, "I shall return! And when I do, those responsible for this villainy shall pay dearly! All of Royal Pond will pay for the disloyalty done me this day!" Then he turned to all the other residents of the pond gathered on water and shore.

"I renounce you all as my subjects! I don't care if the whole pond dries up and the lot of you along with it!"

Theodore turned and walked away over the crest with Jeremy close behind, as thousands of blinking, silent frogs watched them go.

CHAPTER EIGHT

For a space of time Theodore and Jeremy simply walked. Or, Jeremy walked and Theodore hopped, is more accurate. Theodore would hop and Jeremy would race forward to catch up. Then Theodore would hop again and Jeremy would race forward again. Finally Jeremy had to say something.

"Your Majesty?"

"Yes, my good fellow?"

"Could you," (pant, pant) "I mean, do you think you could, (pant, pant), "walk for a while?"

"Walk?"

"Yeah, it's pretty tough trying to keep up. I mean, a hop is a little more than a walk, unless I had longer legs, and then maybe…"

"Oh. Yes, I suppose. I nearly forgot that you're not a frog, like I." Theodore began to walk, which was more like a strut.

"Uh, your Majesty?" Jeremy asked.

"Yes? What? Not slow enough still?"

"No, that's fine, uhm , I was just wondering, uhm, where are we going?"

"To find the Royal Necklace of course! To find the true thieves! The real traitors!"

"Right. Sorry, but, uhm…where IS the necklace?"

"How should I know! Perhaps this "Toad" person has it. Or someone else. I don't know. Someone's got it, and I've got to get it back or else I'll be a commoner all my life. And what worse fate could there be?"

"But, don't you think we ought to know where we're going first? I mean we might end up going everywhere the necklace *isn't*."

The King stopped and looked at Jeremy and frowned.

"Never thought of that."

"Maybe if we knew who wanted it?" Jeremy suggested.

Theodore couldn't believe what he was hearing.

"Wanted it? Wanted it? Ye Gods man! EVERYONE wants it! It's the Royal Necklace! The symbol of Kings!"

"I see. Okay. And, why is that exactly?"

"Well…it's uh…because it's…well obviously it's…it's not important is it? It just IS, you know! Some balderdash about changing something into something else. But it doesn't. Doesn't do anything. Just hangs there getting in the way. Anyway, that's not the point, is it? The point is, it's gone and I'm no longer King!"

Jeremy frowned, hoping he could be a little more helpful than it was being. "Is there somebody who might want to steal the necklace more than anyone else?"

"Oh, well, my Cousin Archie's always wanted the thing. When we were young I'd want to play leap frog and he'd stay behind to stare at it all day. But say, you really don't think he'd steal it do you? I mean, why bother? Though, he does get to be King…there is that, I suppose."

"Could he be hiding it back at the pond?"

"No, no that's impossible. The pond's so

populated there's no place to hide. I could never go anywhere without being whispered about, or pointed at. It's not easy being better than everyone else you know. Always in the public eye…"

"So what you're saying is…the necklace could be anywhere?" Jeremy offered.

"I suppose," Theodore said. And then he stopped walking abruptly. "Gad! It's impossible isn't it?"

"Well…you could sort of say that, your Highness."

Theodore sat down and put his head in his hands. "To think a simple silver chain and a medallion made from green mud, could mean the ruination of my life!"

"Did you say "silver" chain?" Jeremy asked.

"Yes. A silver chain set with a green stone in the center. Oh why me!"

Jeremy jumped to his feet.

"I've seen it!" he shouted. "I've seen the necklace!"

"REALLY!" Theodore said, jumping up.

"Yes! In my village the other day. Two big furry animals came running through town. One had a chain just like that in its mouth! And I…I fought them off…"

Theodore started hopping up and down.

"Ah hah! What a brave fellow!" Theodore shouted. "We'll route the ruddy beggars!" Theodore cried. "Catch 'em in the act! But we have to hurry because at the next full moon my cousin will be crowned King. And if we could do it before supper that would be most convenient because I'm getting frightfully hungry."

"It may take a little longer than that, your Highness."

Just then, a huge shadow passed over them. Jeremy instinctively jumped for cover, leaving the King behind. He found a bush to hide behind and called to the King.

"Run your Highness! A hawk! A hawk!"

"Run?" Theodore said, not understanding. "The King'?... Run?"

A wind sent dust clouds billowing up around them. They both coered their eyes. When the wind stopped, Jeremy was clutching a branch of the bush and Theodore was coughing. Jeremy's tail was stiff and quivering and he couldn't move. A voice from behind made them both jerk.

"If I was a hawk, you'd both be lunch," said the voice.

Theodore and Jeremy turned to see a darkly feathered duck standing behind them. It was Maggie. Jeremy relaxed and dusted himself off, trying to regain some of his dignity.

"We...we...we're NOT afraid of hawks. That's ridiculous. We're just not used to being snuck up on, that's all! We were just getting ready to defend ourselves."

"Looks like you were hiding in the bushes."

"Well it doesn't really matter what you think. Sorry we can't stay and chat, duck, but we have important things to do."

"Like finding the necklace?"

Theodore and Jeremy looked at Maggie suspiciously.

"I live on the pond, too. I hear things. Figured you'd need some help."

"My dear girl," said Theodore sincerely, "this is far too treacherous a quest to involve a female. This is a man's game, don't you know. Calls for quick thinking. Bravery in the face of the enemy…"

"Right. I don't think I could hide in the bushes nearly as well as you boys."

"I wasn't hiding!" Jeremy said, and kicked some dirt.

"I'm female, but I CAN fly, can't I? And I CAN scout ahead, can't I? And I can swim, or walk faster than both of you put together. And I can keep away hawks and owls, can't I?"

Jeremy and Theodore looked at one another. Jeremy's ego was throbbing.

"We don't need you," Jeremy said flatly. "We're doing just fine thanks."

"I say," Theodore put in, "she does have a point."

"What?"

"And she IS a loyal subject of mine, wanting to serve her King. After all, I don't have too many loyal subjects left."

Jeremy kicked the dirt again. "Oh, alright…if his Majesty says so. But, I don't want any dumb "goose" telling me what to do. Or calling me a coward!"

Maggie strode up to Jeremy and put her wing tips on her hips.

"First of all 'whiskers', I'm not a goose. And secondly, if I was your size the only thing I could do against a hawk is run and hide. Unless I was stupid. And I'm not. So, nobody's callin' you anything."

"My name's not 'whiskers."

"Whatever. Do we understand each other?"

"I wasn't scared."

"This is splendid!" Theodore cut in. "Off to find the necklace with two champions at my side. Of course you'll have to do the duties of servants as well. We must keep up the proprieties." He happily rubbed his hands together. "Oh this is marvelous! The lower classes can be so helpful to have around. I don't know what I was thinking."

Maggie cocked one eyebrow at the words 'Servants', and 'Lower Classes'.

Jeremy trailed after Theodore. Theodore continued talking as if it was totally natural for servants to follow him around.

"Come along, champions. We've got a direction now. No time to waste. The culprits will pay dearly, I tell you. Using my necklace for their own abominable purposes. Blast! I'll probably have to send it out for a good cleaning."

Maggie twisted on her heels and waddled after them.

CHAPTER NINE

In their burrow next to a washed out bend in a slow stream, the two moles, Charlie and Irving, sat at a table smoking cigars. The cigars were made of rolled-up dried leaves they'd found outside their burrow in the fall. The leaves made an awful smell, and often caught fire, but smoking them was part of their daily practice. They were practicing to become human. And to the very dim, the worst human habits are always the easiest ones to practice.

The tiny mouse arrow had been removed from Charlie's leg, and needless to say, there was quite a lot of screaming that went on as that was done. Charlie's leg was now bandaged and propped up on a stool next to the table, under a hole in the ceiling which let a small amount of daylight seep directly down in a yellow circle. Charlie let out a puff of smoke.

"I knew we shoulda' gone 'around' 'dat mouse village."

"You did not."

"Did so," Charlie said. "I had a secret plan."

"You didn't have a secret plan, gimme a break!" Irving said, giving him a burning stare.

"Okay... but... if I DID have a secret plan," Charlie said, regretfully. "I would o' gone around them mouses, boy!"

"Ya' know, there's somethin' about mouses," said Irving, suddenly becoming very serious, "Dey' don't blink their eyes, ya' know? Dey' just keep starin', like they know somethin' you don't. I hate dat'. And dey' got those long tails that don't got any hair on 'em. I mean, how scary is that? And, and , and twitchy noses, and.....oh, jeeze, I gotta stop talkin' about it. I'm gonna get, like, nightmares. "

"Yeah, I hate 'dem mouses, boy," Charlie said, taking another deep puff on his cigar. As he sucked in, the end of Charlie's cigar started glowing red hot and suddenly burst into flame. Charlie threw the cigar to the ground and stomped on it violently, unfortunately with the wrong leg.

"Aaahh!", he screamed and fell, landing on the cigar and gripping his bandaged leg. Irving didn't even notice. He went on daydreaming.

"Can't wait to be human," Irving said with a sigh, and Charlie stopped wailing for a moment, as if Irving had just said something very holy.

"Yeah, human," whispered Charlie. Then he sniffed the air. There was smoke coming up all around him.

"Aaugh!" Charlie yelled again, and jumped up from the ground where he'd been sitting on his lit cigar. He ran around the room fanning his smoking tail and yelling each time he landed on his bad leg. Irving kept puffing away, lost in thought.

After Charlie put out the fire by scooting around on the dirt floor, he picked up another of their homemade cigars, lit it as if nothing had happened, and delicately sat back down at the table.

"We won't live in a hole no more," Irving began.

"Guess ya' gotta take the bad wit' the good," Charlie said, nodding his head.

"But," Irving said, pointing a finger in the air, "we can come back and take care of dat' lousy bear for good."

"I'm gonna love 'dat!" said Charlie with a smile.

"Boy, do I hate that bear," said Irving."

"Yeah, me too, boy," Charlie said."

They would have gone on like this all day, as they normally did, if they hadn't been interrupted by a noise coming from the front of the burrow entrance. The noise got louder until they could hear voices.

"Hey! Anybody home?" called a voice.

"Knock, Knock. Who's there?" came another voice.

"Just stick your head in," said yet another voice outside the entrance.

A head-----the head of a raccoon----suddenly popped through the entrance to the burrow. The raccoon head smiled a car-salesman-type smile that showed off his sharp white teeth, a smart pencil moustache.

"Hey, you two! It's me...Danny! I got the boys with me! Thought we'd drop by for a game, eh?" The two moles glanced at each sideways. Danny pulled the rest of himself into the burrow and called to his companions waiting outside.

"Come on in, fella's. The mole brothers is "at 'ome", so to speak."

Charlie turned to Irving and whispered, "Not again. Last time we lost a week's worth of roots."

"They cheat," Irving whispered through his teeth.

"Yeah," Charlie whispered back, "Even better than we do...."

Three other raccoons squeezed through the entrance and faced the two moles. They each had smiles as wide as Danny's.

"You know the boys," Danny said in a gleaming Cockney accent, "Fatbottom, Winkie, and of course, there's old Slick?"

Each of the raccoons bowed in turn.

"What've you boys been up to, eh?" asked Slick. "No good I suppose."

Charlie and Irving looked nervously at one another, horrified that the theft of the necklace might be showing on their faces.

"Nuttin'," said Irving. "Why? What've ya' heard?"

"Just another boring day for us," said Charlie,

nervously. Fatbottom, a sloppy fat raccoon, put a hand on Charlie's shoulder and spoke in rich Shakespearean prose.

"Not anymore cousins. "Let's go see Charlie and Irving", says I. "Why should they suffer the slings and arrows of life alone?", says I. And thus, we bring our mortal coils hence."

Out of nowhere, Danny produced a large bag.

"Lookie, Lookie.....," he said, as if offering a peanut to an elephant. Out of the bag, Danny produced a half-full bottle of yellowish liquid. In large letters the bottle read: "PINEAPPLE JUICE."

"Aged!" Danny announced. "Powerful stuff, mates. Guaranteed!"

Now, of all the creatures the moles mistrusted in the world, the raccoons were at the top of their list. But alcohol, being one of the worst human vices, was irresistible to the moles. They jumped up out of their chairs and ran, Charlie hobbling, over to examine the bottle. Fatbottom seized this as an opportunity to grab an empty chair and sat down at the table making himself comfortable. The chair creaked under the strain.

Irving grabbed the bottle of pineapple juice and both moles sniffed it. They went cross-eyed, which was a good thing in their estimation. It was indeed old and fermented. Powerful stuff.

"Anything to munch on?" Slick asked in his

nasally voice, smacking his lips.

"Mmmm, I'm fah-fah- fah... famished!" Winkie said. Winkie's twitch was in full force.

Irving put the bottle behind his back.

"Nope, we're all out," Irving lied. "Heavens, what shall we do?"

"Sorry," said Charlie, "how remiss of us, not to have a thing to offer our guests. What a terrible shame. Oh well, better come back another time when we're all stocked up," he said, as both he and Irving tried to usher Danny out the entrance. Slick slid open a drawer at the rear of the burrow and produced out a handful of roots.

"Look what I found!" Slick exclaimed, in a voice that sounded a little like he had a bee in his nose.

"Mmm..." said Fatbottom, patting his fat stomach, "I do feel a bit peckish..."

"Wait a minute," Charlie said, desperately, "if we're gonna play cards, Irving an' I'll need those roots to bet with. It's all we got."

"Zounds, I suppose we can't take a fellow's betting money, eh, Slick?" said Fatbottom.

"Have a seat, gentlemen," Danny said, motioning to the table and chairs. He slicked down the greasy but neatly parted hair on the top of his head and took a seat himself.

"Dealer's choice, I believe," he said, and turned over his hand revealing a deck of cards.

"We came with full purse, cousins," Fatbottom said. "Beware."

"Just look!" Slick said, "shinies!" With that, he produced a bag which he dumped out on the table. Shiny rocks, broken glass, some silver coins and some bottle caps fell out in a heap. Charlie and Irving were immediately hypnotized by the twinkling objects.

"You guh-guh-guh-guh-got any shinies, mates?" Winkie asked Charlie and Irving.

"We got the best shiny you ever-burhhbb!" Charlie began until Irving slapped a hand over his mouth just in time.

"Nope!" Irving said, "just roots. Dat's all."

Irving gave Charlie an icepick glare.

Under the table, Charlie checked the bandages on his leg and reached beneath the bandages to glimpse of the shiny green necklace hidden there. Assured the necklace was safe, Charlie stuffed it back down into the bandages.

Slick, as clever a pickpocket as ever lived in the animal kingdom, did not miss this going's on. His shifty eyes darted back and forth between Charlie and Irving.

The card game progressed with smoke filling the room, and the animals betting heavily with food and shiny objects. The raccoons were smoking cigars too, and made sure that Charlie and Irving drank as much fermented pineapple juice as possible. Before long, the two moles were singing, swaying in their chairs, and sloshing the juice all about the table top. The raccoons laughed and patiently bided their time.

"Another round of drinks!" called Slick.

"Another down of rinks!" echoed Irving.

"Another . . . HICCUP! Hee, hee, hee" said Charlie, laughing stupidly. Not able to resist stupid laughter, Irving joined in as well.

While the moles were laughing hysterically, the raccoons pretended to drink again and again, but somehow their glasses never had to be refilled. The bottle made its way around to the moles once more.

Fatbottom stood and made a toast.

"To our cousins!"

"To our cousins!" the Raccoons all repeated..

Irving and Charlie stood up. The room was spinning around and it was hard for them to keep up with it. Irving took another giant swig out of the bottle and handed it to Charlie.

"To our cousins!" they both said, their tongues now seeming to have minds of their own.

Without warning, Irving's eyes crossed, his jaw dropped, he shook a bit, and keeled straight over backwards.

Charlie was barely able to stand up himself. Seeing double, he lifted the bottle into the air to resume the toast.

"To our...to the...hey, who let all these raccoons in here?" He squinted, trying to clear his vision of the twenty raccoons that now stood at the table. "Is there a party?" he asked. Then something occurred to him, "It must be my birthday!" he said and began to hug himself immodestly. A very wide grin spread across his face, his eyes crossed, and down he went joining his brother on the floor.

Slick got up and pulled the necklace from Charlie's bandages. FatBottom laughed a hoarse laugh and took another puff on his cigar.

"Toad should be surprised, me thinks," he said.

"Ya-ya-you sure this is guh-guh-gonna work?" Winkie asked.

"Toad's not the sort 'o bloke I'd wanna cross," Slick said.

"Don't worry boys," Danny said, as he took the necklace from Slick, "Toad's gone to a lot of trouble for this. He won't care how he gets it. My guess is he'll pay plenty. Yep, mi'lads, this is our ticket to paradise!"

He held up the necklace in the light from above. It twinkled and gleamed a beautiful green and silver as the four raccoons gazed at it with their dark bandit eyes.

CHAPTER TEN

The next day Theodore, Jeremy and Maggie were making their way along the edge of a sandy creek bed. Jeremy was in the lead, reading tracks as he went.

"Look," Maggie began, "explain this to me. If we've lost the trail, why are we going on?"

"They were headed this way," Jeremy answered, never taking his eyes off the ground. "We'll find the trail any time now."

"What happens if we do find 'em? Most big furry animals have big sharp teeth, you know."

Jeremy whirled around and waved his arms in the air. "What's the matter? Scared?"

"Yes," Maggie said. "What's the big deal about bein' scared? Everybody gets scared."

"Not me!" Jeremy shouted angrily.

"What's your problem anyway? I know people don't like me, but you were like this before I met you."

"Never mind!" Jeremy said and resumed his tracking.

"A woman, I believe," Theodore said distractedly. He was looking for flies.

Jeremy spun around again. "How do you know!"

"You talk in your sleep, dear fellow," Theodore

said just before his tongue shot out and grabbed a fly. "Of course, my hearing is quite exceptional. I am a frog, after all."

Jeremy kicked the dirt and continued on. "I wanted to marry her, but she said I wasn't brave enough. I'll prove I'm brave. Then she'll be sorry. She want me back again and...and I won't have anything to do with her!"

"She pretty?" Maggie asked.

"Yeah."

"So, it's okay for somebody to make a fool out of you as long as they're beautiful, right? Then you'll go back and make a fool out of yourself again, just because she's pretty. Then she'll find another way ta' make a fool out o' you an'--"

"Stop saying that!" shouted Jeremy, but there was no stopping Maggie now.

"If I ever got the chance, I'd make 'em pay...the pretty ones. Pay in a way that hurts 'em most. The way they look. Turn 'em into somethin' so ugly they never could dream of it. Hideous... that's the word... I'd make 'em so hideous no one would believe it. Then let 'em call people names."

Jeremy and Theodore had stopped walking and stood staring at Maggie. Maggie suddenly realized she'd said too much.

"You don't know what it's like to be ugly."

"Are you ugly?" asked Theodore.

"Well, 'course. You blind?" she answered.

"You look like a normal duck to me," Jeremy said, examining her feathers closely.

Suddenly the sun disappeared. A shadow circled them on the ground. Jeremy froze.

"A hawk!" he said, his teeth chattering.

"Scatter!!" Maggie shouted.

Jeremy and Maggie ran for cover. Theodore stood out in plain sight, his fists raised to the sky.

"Coward!" he yelled. "Come down and I'll give you the thrashing you deserve!"

Jeremy skidded to a halt and saw the hawk diving for Theodore. He was out in the open too. He tried to move but his legs were locked.

The hawk swooped by, barely missing Theodore. Theodore, with hands on hips, kept taunting the great bird.

Jeremy still couldn't move. His tail was stiff as a stick and quivering.

With the hawk's next pass it swooped in, missing Theodore, who ducked, but, continuing on, it grabbed Jeremy's stiff tail instead, lifting the mouse into the air.

"HELP! -- HELP!" Jeremy shouted.

The hawk stared down with hungry eyes at Jeremy as the mouse struggled in the great bird's talons. The hawk ran his tongue along his curved beak and was about to tear the mouse into pieces, when the hawk was struck by something hard. The blow sent the hawk's head spinning, and it opened it's talons. A hundred feet in the air, Jeremy was tumbling head over heels, heading for the hard earth below.

"He-e-e-l-l-l-p-p!" he yelled as he dropped faster and faster. The end was coming. He knew it. He pressed his eyes closed waiting for the ground to come. Then, inches before the hard earth, Jeremy was magically scooped up and whisked into the air.

The hawk, who had been tumbling right behind Jeremy, hit the ground with a "WHOOF" of feathers and dust. It lay on the ground, eyes crossed and wings all twisted.

Jeremy was dropped onto his feet on the bank of the stream. It was only then that he looked up.

It was Maggie.

"Stay low," she said in a whisper, "and be still until he leaves." Jeremy was shaking too much to reply.

The hawk got to its feet, stumbled a few times, and made a dizzy takeoff.

"The King!" Jeremy suddenly remembered. "Where's the King?"

"Over here, chaps!" Theodore chimed, with a pleasant smile. "Brilliant show, what?"

The duck and mouse followed the voice to a large rock in the middle of the stream. Theodore was waving at them.

"Jolly good show, Maggie, girl! Splendid play!"

Maggie bowed. Theodore hopped from rock to rock.

"Wish I'd been close enough to clout the rascal myself. I say, Jeremy, thought you were "done in" for a moment there."

Jeremy was so furious he began jumping up and down and waving his arms like a lunatic.

"I'll give you the thrashing you deserve? What's wrong with you! You're just a frog! That hawk could have killed you! What happens to Royal Pond if you get killed!!"

Theodore's pleasant smile retreated. Jeremy then turned his rage on Maggie.

"And I didn't need any help!"

"Is that right?" Maggie asked calmly.

"That's right! I was doing just fine!"

Jeremy trounced away over the edge of the bank down into a washed-out turn in the creek bed.

CHAPTER ELEVEN

Some time later, Jeremy was trudging along the creek bed talking to himself.

"I'm not a coward...I'm not coward...I'm not...." The mouse stopped and leaned against the wall of the washed out creek bank. "I'm not a coward. I'm not. I can't be..."

Just then, a trickle of dirt began falling on his head. Then more dirt. He quickly dove out of the way as a dark furry animal came tumbling out of a hole in the bank.

Irving spilled out of their burrow and hit the stream with a SPLASH!

Jeremy scrambled up the bank as fast as his little legs would go. Maggie and Theodore were trailing just behind, and, seeing the creatures for themselves, quickly joined Jeremy on the top of the stream bank.

Irving sat in the stream holding his head. His eyes were baggy and bloodshot. A bird sang a song and he covered his ears in pain.

"Ahh!"

The next moment, Charlie came hurling out of the burrow entrance, falling on top of Irving. Charlie got to his feet in the rushing water and stumbled around with his arms outstretched, eyes sealed shut.

"I can't see! I'm blind! I can't see the sky! I'm blind I tell ya'! Blind! What did I do to deserve this!"

Irving emerged from the mud, coughing and gasping for air. He saw Charlie stumbling in the stream in front of him and kicked at Charlie's legs. Charlie's body slapped back down into the water. He came up coughing and blinking his eyes.

"I can see! I can see! It's a miracle!" He turned to Irving, grabbed his head, gave him a big kiss and hugged him cheek to cheek. "Funny how it's the little things that mean so much..."

"Get off me, you stooge!" Irving said, pushing his brother away. Then they both just sat there in the water, staring at nothing, water rushing around them, as their brains slowly got back into motion.

"Those lousy raccoons!" Charlie said. "I'll bet they took off with our food again." He laid back down in the water and threw a splashing tantrum.

"Dey' do it every time!" Irving cried.

Charlie suddenly sat up. He fumbled around for the necklace under his bandages and froze. Irving stared at him. Charlie slowly pulled out his hand. It was empty.

"Ahhh!" they both screamed. They both collapsed back into the stream, beating the water in side by side tantrums.

Above the moles' burrow, Jeremy, Maggie and

Theodore were still lying flat to the ground, watching.

"That's them," Jeremy whispered. "The ones I saw with the necklace."

"You sure? They don't act like they're the sharpest needles in the haystack," whispered Maggie.

Charlie and Irving, wet and miserable, crawled slowly back into their burrow. They were still sobbing and lamenting their misfortune and slapping at each other as they climbed the bank.

"It was all your fault," said one.

"Shut up!" said the other. "Mom was right. You're a big dope!"

"Shut up! Mom always said I had potential!"

"Yeah. Ta' be a big dope!"

"Did not....."

"Did so..." And so forth all the way into their burrow.

Maggie paced in circles on the bank, thinking.

"We gotta get 'em to tell us where that necklace is," she said. Then, she stopped and stared at the ground with her mouth open.

"What is it?" Jeremy asked.

"Look," she whispered, pointing with a wing.

She gestured to a small hole in the ground in front of her. Jeremy and Theodore bent low to examine it. Jeremy put his eye to the hole and peered in.

Down below, Jeremy could see the two moles as they sat at their table, holding their heads and moaning. They were still slapping at each other whenever they remembered how upset they were.

Theodore wasn't paying any attention. He was on the edge of the bank a few feet away. As the orange sun set, he had noticed his shadow on the opposite stream bank. The frog shadow was enormous. He made the giant shadow dance and jump and wave its fearful arms.

Jeremy sat up. He was trying to think of a plan. He saw Theodore waving his arms to make the shadow on the opposite bank do a lovely dance.

"Look at him," Jeremy said, shaking his head. "He doesn't care about anything. You'd think he was on a picnic."

"There's gotta be a way to get 'em to talk," said Maggie.

"Right. I'll just go down and ask 'em," Jeremy said sarcastically.

Jeremy looked at Theodore again, who was making scary gestures with his shadow. The shadow was a frightening shape against the opposite bank, Jeremy had to admit. He looked back at the hole. He looked up at Maggie.

"I've got an idea. . ."

"Should I be scared?" she asked.

CHAPTER TWELVE

The moles were sitting at their table inside their burrow lamenting their rotten luck when suddenly the burrow went dark. The moles' eyes glowed brightly in the darkness. A voice echoed through the burrow.

"I HAVE COME!" said the booming voice. "I AM THE FROG GOD, AND I HAVE COME FOR MY NECKLACE!"

The moles looked around frantically until both of them locked their eyes on the entrance, and the monstrous shadow beyond the creek.

"THE THIEVES WILL SOON KNOW MY VENGEANCE!" boomed the voice.

The moles flew into each other's arms and backed up to the far wall.

"We... don't got it no more!" Charlie whined through chattering teeth.

"Yeah," said Irving, shivering, "the... the... Raccoons! They stole it!"

The Frog God's voice thundered inside the burrow. "WHERE IS THE NECKLACE! IF YOU LIE I WILL DESTROY YOU!"

The shadow across the stream made two great fists and shook them.

"No! No!" Charlie cried, "you don't gotta destroy us! They're downstream! They're from downstream! The raccoons! At the Dumping Place!"

"Yeah," Irving squeaked, "dat's right...We don't

got it! They're the ones who got it! Go destroy them!

"WE SHALL SEE...," said the voice. "BUT IF YOU ARE LYING I WILL BE BACK...AND DESTROY YOU COMPLETELY!" The voice echoed through the burrow as the two moles pressed back even flatter against the wall.

Maggie pulled her head out of the hole and light came into the burrow once more. Jeremy gestured with an "OK" sign.

Down below, Charley and Irving stared at each other with mouths gaping wide.

"He could even make duh' sun go away..." said Irving in awe.

"Whoa..." is all Charlie could say.

Maggie bowed and gestured a wing to Theodore. Theodore, walking up from the bank, took three or four bows for his performance.

CHAPTER THIRTEEN

Jeremy, Theodore, and Maggie were making their way down the creek bank toward the Dumping Place until late that evening. Theodore had been silent for much of the time.

"I suppose he would be a frog," Theodore finally said to no one in particular.

"Who?" Maggie asked.

"God. Being "supreme" and all. What else could he be but a frog?"

Theodore started hopping and took the lead. He could only take so much deep thinking at a time. He had learned to ration it.

"And you want this guy ta' be King?" Maggie asked Jeremy.

Jeremy just smirked and shook his head.

CHAPTER FOURTEEN

It was raining when Jeremy, drenched and cold, led Maggie and Theodore down a muddy hill. Theodore was in his glory in the rain. Maggie seemed to be enjoying herself too, but Jeremy was miserable.

Lightning flashed. Thunder followed.

After an hour of sloshing through the mud, they came to a bridge where huge metal monsters with burning eyes rolled passed on an black river. The black river had white lines on it and the metal monsters raced down one side or the other of the lines. It was, of course, a road.

As the three reached the edge of the road, the rain abruptly stopped. Clouds parted to display a bright half moon. Cars and trucks, their headlights flaring, barreled down the road that had now become a shimmering yellow path in the moonlight.

"I suppose we should just wait until one of these things goes by and then run across," Jeremy said, shivering.

"My feathers are too wet to fly," Maggie said.

As they stood pondering how to cross the road, they failed to notice the change in their companion. Theodore had been staring at the glimmering road ever since the moon came out. His eyes were wide and empty and he was grinning stupidly. It was as if he were a child staring at a giant ice cream Sunday.

Theodore walked out onto the road.

"I think we should go one at a time," Jeremy said to Maggie. "That way if anyone gets hit...," he swallowed, "...the other two can go on."

"All right," Maggie said, "you can go first. That way the King can - hey," she looked around, "where is he?"

Maggie caught motion out of the corner of her eye. She turned to see Theodore near the center of the road, weaving around as if he were dizzy. Jeremy pivoted to look and cringed as a car shot passed the frog, just missing him.

Jeremy's tail started to quiver.

A big-rig truck came zooming down the road taking up more space than the road provided. Maggie flapped backwards, off the road, but Jeremy panicked and ran out into the road. He spun like a top in the wind as a the truck's monstrous tires missed him by inches.

Theodore was on the center line now, doing some kind of dance. Jeremy spotted another car coming at Theodore and raced pull him out of the way. He got to Theodore just in time, and pulled. The car whipped passed. Jeremy grabbed the frog by the shoulders and shook him.

"What are you doing! You wanna get killed!"

"Come in! Come in!" said Theodore, with wild

eyes, "but everyone must wear a hat!"

Jeremy froze again as he caught sight of another oncoming truck.

"Wonderful tea party, eh?" Theodore continued. "Anyone for crochet?"

Theodore danced off, down the white center line, the moonlight casting a slender shadow behind his pudgy body. The truck came at them and Jeremy ducked. The truck whizzed passed, missing them both. He turned and yelled.

"Your Highness! We've got to get outtah' here!" Jeremy screamed. "Come on!"

The mouse ran and grabbed Theodore's arm and began tugging. Theodore's slippery frog arm slid out of Jeremy's grasp just as another car's tires cut the space between them like a knife.

"On with the show!" Theodore shouted. "Start the music! Light the footlights!" Theodore's eyes seemed to focus on something as he gazed down the road at the approaching headlights. He blinked and rubbed his eyes.

Down the road, coming straight for him, were lines and lines of cabaret singers. They all look just like Gypsy with big red lips. The singers were doing chorus-line kicks, making their way to Theodore. Theodore was horrified.

"Ahh! They're coming to get me!" he screamed in terror.

Cars continued to whiz by. The road was so wet that every time tires would pass, they were drenched by a wall of water.

"Maggie!" Jeremy yelled.

Theodore started twirling round and round. In his trance, he was in the middle of the chorus line. The chorus of cabaret singers was enveloping him, making him the center of their show.

Jeremy froze as another car shot by him. The wind from the car blew him, skidding on his behind, right over to Theodore.

Theodore wasn't afraid anymore. In his dream he was now the center of the show. Spotlights, the headlights of the cars, were shining on him and the audience cheered as the chorus of girl frogs danced all around him. He thought Jeremy was one of the dancers in the chorus and took the mouse's hands, dancing gaily this way and that as four more deadly wheels went whizzing by.

"You dance divinely, my dear," Theodore said, charmingly, his eyes spinning. He left Jeremy and was carried away by the imaginary chorus girls again.

"No!" shouted Jeremy.

Jeremy ran for Theodore again, dodging in and out of tires and spewing water. He finally got hold of the frog's coat and started dragged the frog across the slippery road. Theodore tried desperately to get loose.

"Wait! Wait! The finale! Mumsie's bringing pudding! And we can't leave without desert!"

Just then, a giant truck appeared in front of them. The instant they were about to be smashed flat, they were both lifted off the ground and thrown toward the side of the road. This was followed by a thick "THUD" sound which went unnoticed as Jeremy and Theodore went tumbling down over the muddy road bank.

Jeremy, panting heavily, crawled to Theodore, who was lying sprawled on his back. The mouse grabbed the King by the lapels of his coat and stuck his face down into Theodore's and gritted his teeth.

"I dance divinely my dear! Mumsie's bringing PUDDING!" Jeremy repeated, gritting his teeth as his mouse hair stood on end. Then he collapsed onto his back in the mud.

The spinning of Theodore's eyes had ceased. He blinked and shook his wide head.

"That... must be a what they call a 'road'" he said, gasping for air. "My Uncle Louie crossed a road once."

"Well, then he... he should have warned you!" Jeremy said, in between panting for air.

"Couldn't do it, you see. He's been hanging on

one of the walls of the palace for years, poor devil. Flat as a pancake. Uncle Arthur. Art for short."

"What? You hang him up and call him--" just then Jeremy bolted upright.

"Oh my gosh! Maggie!"

The moon cast ghostly shadows on the slippery roadside now as the frog and mouse crawled back up the bank toward the road. Jeremy turned to Theodore.

"You look the other way this time!"

Theodore turned around and sat facing away from the road. His eyes flared in alarm.

"Oh...heavens no! "

Jeremy turned to look at what Theodore was seeing. There, off to the side of the road, feathers plastered down by mud, lay Maggie.

CHAPTER FIFTEEN

In the morning sunlight Maggie laid in the mud with her eyes closed. Jeremy and Theodore had dragged her under a tree not far from where cars and trucks were still streaming passed. Feathers dusted the ground around her and one of her wings was slightly bent.

"Maggie?" Theodore asked, timidly.

Jeremy was stroking the feathers on her head.

"Wake up, Maggie," Jeremy whispered.

A big tear rolled off Theodore's cheek, he sniffled a few times and turned away. Jeremy's eyes were swimming in tears, too. He knew it wasn't what someone brave might do, but he couldn't help it.

Without the two noticing, Maggie's eyes slowly and weakly opened.

"What happened?" she asked softly.

Wiping his eyes, Jeremy looked down at Maggie. A huge smile of relief spread across his face.

"Oh, Maggie!" he exclaimed.

Theodore turned and, seeing Maggie alive, threw his arms around her. Jeremy, too, started hugging her around the neck.

Maggie looked confused. Nothing made sense to her yet and it made her frightened. In spite of their pleading, she would not lay still, and clumsily she got to her feet. She staggered a bit and moaned when she tried to move her right wing. It was broken.

"Did I get hit?" Maggie asked.

"We...we thought you were dead," Jeremy said wiping his face.

"Are you... cryin'?" she asked, still confused.

"You were hurt. We thought you were...."

"You... you're cryin' because of me?"

"Well, you're our friend, dear girl, of course," said Theodore, wiping his own eyes. "And...I...I can't help it, you see."

Jeremy smiled helplessly.

"You're both cryin' because of me?" she asked again in disbelief. "Your friend?"

They both nodded. She waited a long time before she said anything.

"Never had a friend before," she said very quietly.

"Nor I," Theodore replied without thinking. "Oh, how embarrassing," he said, half-laughing, and wiping his eyes.

Jeremy composed himself and cleared his throat.

"We have to put a splint on that," he said, pointing to her wing. "Come on your Highness. Let's find some sticks and something to tie them with."

"Right you are! You rest here, my dear. You'll be as good as new in no time at all."

As her friends marched off, Maggie stared at them in wonder.

"Cryin' because of me?" she whispered.

CHAPTER SIXTEEN

Inside their burrow, Charlie and Irving were working by candle light. There was a storm brewing outside. Lightning flashed every once in a while and the "boom" that came afterward made the two moles jerk.

Each time there was a flash, crude drawings appeared on the walls of the burrow. They were faces. They were drawings of frog faces in chalk. Charlie and Irving had been busy drawing the faces for the last two days.

To Charlie and Irving, if the Frog God ever returned with the idea of destroying them completely, he might be more forgiving if he saw they had turned it into a kind of Frog God Temple.

Irving stepped back and looked at his most recent frog face. Charlie stopped and looked too. It was a terrible drawing, with one frog eye bigger than the other, and the mouth crooked.

"Now dat's a good lookin' frog, boy," he said, admiring the chalk outline.

Another flash of lightning came, and a black shape appeared within the chalk outline Irving had just drawn. It was the black outline of a frog's head. They stared at the wall in horror as another jagged thread of lightning flashed and the dark shape of the frog became more clear.

In panic, they scurried to the side wall, running back and forth, stumbling into each other.

"What are you doing, you idiots!" Archibald said as he stepped into the candle light. The two moles stared at Archibald and sighed in relief.

"Whew!" sighed Irving, "We thought it was...you know...'HIM'."

"Yeah," said Charlie, spreading his hands wide, " 'HIM'."

"What are you blabbering on about?"

"The Frog God," Irving said in a whisper.

"The what?"

"The Frog God," said Charlie, looking from side to side as if something were about to pop out of the walls. "He came for duh' necklace. He was really ticked off, boy."

"You didn't give it to him did you!"

"No," said Irving.

"Whew! Thank goodness," said Archibald with a sigh of relief.

"Duh' raccoons already took it," Charlie said.

"WHAT! YOU FOOLS! Do you mean to tell me you no longer have the necklace?"

They both shook their heads.

"Good thing too, boy" Irving began, "duh' Frog God would o' destroyed us completely."

"Yep," Charlie said eagerly, "dat's what he said. "We'd be destroyed completely". Wait till the Frog

God catches up wid' them raccoons, boy," Charlie giggled. "Hah! Serve 'em right." They both started chuckling in evil little mole chuckles.

"We just been makin' pictures in case duh' Frog God comes back. He'd feel right at home now. In fact, it'd be kind of a rotten shame if he don't come back to see what we done."

"Shut up!" Irving hissed. "What are ya? Ignorant?" Irving looked at Charlie and shoved him. He turned to Archibald.

"We ain't been doin' this the whole time. Sometimes we stop and play each other Solitaire. I'm winnin'," Irving said proudly.

Archie closes his eyes. His lips were quivering with frustration. "How can you play solitaire if you-oh, never mind!" He moved within an inch of their faces. "Are you telling me that some "raccoons" have MY necklace?"

Irving nodded his head.

"Yeah. Unless..."

"Unless what?"

"Unless they decided to sell it," Charlie blurted out.

Archibald's green face turned a roasty crimson.

"SELL IT? TO WHOM?"

"Um...," said Charlie, looking at Irving for help.

"Well...Toad," Irving said with a gulp. Archibald dropped his monocle.

"Don't be stupid! There is no such person. Not anymore at least."

"Yeah there is," said Charlie, "an' he's pretty scary, too."

"Oh he's mean, boy," Irving added. "But he said he'd get us all the roots and shinies we could ever want. And he said he could turn us into humans better than you." Charlie nodded. Archie began to pace back and forth near the entrance. He was very shaken.

"But it can't be Toad." he said, half to himself, "Toad was banished from Royal Pond long before...well, before I was born. Toad, alive?"

Archibald put his hands behind his back and pursed his lips. "He's got spies everywhere," Irving said, looking around.

"And he said he could actually 'change' you?" asked Archibald.

"Yeah, plus, protection from a certain thing with large teeth that I'd rather not mention right now on account of it gives us the willies, if ya' know what I mean."

"And just how did he propose to do this?"

"With the necklace," Charlie said. "He said if we got the necklace for him, he'd turn us into humans right then and there."

They both nodded.

"There's just one tiny little thing he forgot to tell

you though," Archibald said, motioning them forward with one webbed finger. The two moles crept forward until they were within inches of the frogs face again.

"IT DOESN'T WORK!" Archibald screamed. The moles flew back against the cave wall. "It's just a myth! A symbol! And even if it DID work, only someone who has the blood of the Great Frog in his veins could make it work properly!"

"But he told us he had this "thing" he was gonna do to it ta' make it work," Charlie said. He looked to Irving, "What'd he call that thing?"

"Oh, I know! I know!" said Irving, raising his hand and jumping up and down. Then he stopped, "Naahh. I don't know..."

"MMmmmm.....," Archibald began, "he was said to be a genius. I wonder... At any rate," he went on, whirling on the moles, "even if he gets it to work, he can't use it. Unless you return the necklace to me, you'll never become human. Never! Do you understand? Am I -speak-ing slow-ly e-nough? Oh, why am I wasting my time! Pond moss has more intelligence than both of you combined! And what's this lunacy about a Frog God?"

"He was there," said Irving, pointing through the entrance to the far bank of the creek bed.

"He was like a big shadow," said Charlie.

"A shadow, you say?

"Yeah, dat's right, but big!" Irving said. "Really big! With a big ole' head and big bug eyes!"

"Yeah, like you!" added Charlie. "Only bigger."

Both moles nodded. Charlie spread his arms in an attempt to show just how big it was. Archibald sneered at them, then began to consider something.

"Hmm... go on," Archibald said, "and what did this shadow say?"

"Well," began Charlie, scrunching up his face to draw upon his limited brainpower, "he wanted to know where the necklace was. So, we told him the raccoons took it."

Archibald slowly replaced his monocle and looked toward the entrance.

"My Cousin is more clever than I gave him credit," he said, walking to the edge of the entrance. He turned and faced the mole brothers.

"If you two ever hope to become human, you had better find that necklace. Otherwise, you'll live out the rest of your miserable lives being the stupid, overgrown, dirt-digging rats you are now. And...you must do it before the full moon, or you get nothing! Is that clear?"

He turned, and was about to leave. He turned back again. "And there's a certain bear around the pond that might enjoy being shown where to look for a mole pudding....or two."

And with that, Archibald hopped out the

entrance and disappeared.

"Man!!," Irving cried, pulling out his hair, "DAT' BEAR KNOWS EVERYBODY!!!

CHAPTER SEVENTEEN

The raccoons; Danny, Winkie, FatBottom and Slick entered a large dilapidated wooden building almost hidden amongst towering piles of rusting junk and heaps of garbage. Each of them looked nervously about as they entered the doorway. Winkie was twitching at about twice his normal rate.

"This place guh-guh-guh-gives me the shakes."

Further inside, they came to a massive metal canister with thick wires coming out of its sides. It looked like a metal spider. A yellow sign on it read: "ELECTICAL TRANSFORMER-DANGER", and the air around it smelled oily and tart. The piles of wood, glass bottles, and brick took on an eerie architecture as a small trickle of water ran down one end of the rubble to make a waterfall.

"You boys get the feeling we're being watched," Danny said nervously. He spun around quickly, but saw nothing. They walked on, but as soon as their backs were turned, hundreds of blinking yellow eyes appeared from dark crevices behind them.

As the raccoons rounded a corner made of oils cans, they saw stretched before them a miniature city. Colored lights, rats, and voles were busy building an elevator. Lizards were riding an electric train, carrying batteries. Bats were flying in and out of the light, possums were hammering nails while hanging upside down, and colored lights twinkled everywhere in the shack coming from the strands of Christmas lights running in crisscrossing strings above.

Several bats appeared and flitted down in front of FatBottom's face. He tried to swat them but his furry paws only seemed to find empty air. Finally he connected with one and sent it hurling against an empty milk can. The bat hit the can with a "bong" and slid like a piece of wet baloney to the ground.

At the far end of the city was a water fountain. The fountain was a statue of a woman cupping her hands in front of her. Water cascaded from a vase she was carrying on her shoulder. In the statue's hands sat a very large, very fat, Toad.

Little brown frogs and gray mice scurried all around Toad, as the raccoons approached the fountain. Two possums, hanging upside down and carrying large pointy knitting needles barred the way as the raccoons approached.

"Let them pass," came a croaking voice from the fountain.

The four approached the statue slowly, looking from side to side as if at any moment something could jump out and swallow them whole.

The incredibly fat Toad slid to the front of the statue's hands, sloshing water as he did, and looked down at the raccoons.

"What a surprise," he croaked, "the Raccoons. I'm quite beside myself to have such distinguished guests. Strange to see you here, though. I recall a rather large gambling debt you owe me. But here you are, bold as you please."

Too frightened to say anything intelligent, FatBottom pulled the necklace out of his pocket and held it up for Toad to see. They knew they had succeeded in their task when they saw Toad's eyes nearly pop out of his head. The necklace shimmered in the colored light and seemed to draw Toad into it. FatBottom quickly put it away in his coat pocket again.

"We thought," Danny began, "the boys 'n me, that this necklace might be important to you, Toad. It wasn't easy getting it, ya' know."

"Yeah, and we've got expuh-puh-puh-penses you know," Winkie blurted out.

"Oh...of course, expenses.....I see," said Toad. "And just how did you come by this necklace?"

Fatbottom stepped forward and cleared his throat. He had a way of talking that somehow made whatever he said sound prepared, even though most of what he said was made up on the spot.

"Pray you, sir, look at it this way. Without us

there wouldn't be-no-necklace, no how. Besides, it must be worth a great deal. You wanting it so bad, and all."

"Right, you wa-wa-wa-wanting it so bad and all." Winkie added.

"I see," said the Toad. "So you're here to, how do they say it, "Put the squeeze on me?"

"It's just business, Toad, old boy," Danny said.

Like a great sea serpent rising from the pools of shadows behind them, a snake's head rose up in back of the four raccoons. Toad smiled.

"Oh Pierre, it seems these "businessmen" have stolen something I already had plans to steal myself. What do you think we should do?"

Pierre, a long fat rattlesnake, slithered in from the shadows and rattled his tail a few times. The Raccoons slowly turned around. Pierre hissed. Pierre liked the sound of his rattles, but they never seemed to be as frightening as a good hiss. He supposed that was why cats tried to imitate the sound whenever they could. But the imitation was never as good as the real thing.

"Pierre's my "major domo", so to speak. Takes care of the, "little things" I never seem to get around to. He has a terrible temper, too. French, you know. He especially becomes irritated when he feels someone is trying to mislead me. But then, perhaps these fellows were simply playing a trick on old

Toadie, eh Pierre?"

"Yeah, that's right," said Slick, petrified by Pierre, "Just a trick!"

"All in fun!" said Danny.

"A joke, that's all, sir," Fatbottom said, cringing. "Laughter being the noblest of--"

"Pierre," Toad cut in, "bring me the necklace, please."

The snake slithered forward, his ribbon tongue flicking out and in, as he got within inches of Fatbottom's shivering hand. Pierre hooked the necklace on one fang, and slithered up the far side of the fountain. He slithered over the shoulder of the statue and placed the necklace into Toad's waiting hands. Toad pulled it to him and examined it in awe.

"I've waited a lifetime for you," he said to the necklace, reverently. "But now it's all worth it."

"How 'bout something for our trouble, Gov'nuh'!" pleaded Danny. "After all, we bro' it all this way just ta' give it to yuh'."

"Yes, "to give it to me" is, I think the operative phrase," replied Toad.

"Be a sport, Toad! The boys and me deserve a little something, right?" said Slick.

Toad began snapping his fingers.

"Pilar, Hector, Miguel, do we have a little something to give these deserving gentlemen?"

The three bats, Hector, Miguel, and Pilar appeared from a high dark corner of the shack and flapped over to the statue. Miguel landed on the statue's head, the other two on each shoulder. Miguel stretched his wings impressively.

"Sure, Boss, we could like...think of something, you know..."

Pilar sniffed the air, wrinkled her pug nose, and looked at Miguel.

"Hey," she said, "don't chu' believe in deodorant or sometheen'?"

"Huh?" said Miguel. And he stuck his own pug nose into his arm pits. He breathed deeply.

"Smells like springtime."

"Springtime in the sewer. You're so stupid, ju' don't even know."

"Uh huhm..." Toad grumbled, making his jowls quivver. "Normally anyone who tried to cheat me would be killed immediately…"

Pierre hissed and flicked his pointed tongue.

"...but I'm in a wonderful mood today, and killing you would make such a mess." Toad studied the necklace intently. "Pierre, show them the way out, won't you. I shall be busy..."

Pierre began slithering down the fountain, an evil look in his snaky orange eyes.

The raccoons started backing out, then broke into a run. Pouring himself off the fountain, Pierre struck at the four raccoons, dripping poison venom from each of his razor-sharp fangs. Pierre kept striking, missing them by inches, and thinking that if he did bite one, it wouldn't make Toad very upset. And it might make him feel better to get rid of some venom. Storing up venom always gave him a stuffy nose and a headache.

Toad motioned with his arms and the bats fluttered down. They grabbed him by the shoulders and gently lowered him off the fountain, his flabby skin stretched to its limits as his lower half was pulled hard by gravity.

Once down, he made his way over to a platform above the great metal transformer. Tubes and wires crackled and bubbled all around him. Toad looked at the heavy cables that stuck out from the transformer. They came up to either side of the platform. Each end of the cable exposed thick copper wire in the shape of hooks. Toad spoke adoringly to the necklace.

"Soon, my lovely, your power will be restored and together won't we have fun!"

He laughed wildly as he held up the necklace. A ball of electricity sprang to life between the great copper hooks as the sound of his ghoulish laughter echoed the shack.

CHAPTER EIGHTEEN

It was morning. The sun had just come up as frog, mouse, and duck walked in a line to a small sign reading: DUMPTOWN.

Before them, steam rose off enormous mountains of garbage making them look like dirty volcanoes. Well-established foot paths wound their way through the mess and led off into the distance.

Before mid-day, as they made their way through the mountains of trash, they came upon a small mouse village. Homes were made of matchboxes, or empty soup cans. The mice were all shabbily dressed and hid as the three travelers entered.

An old mouse with a white beard approached them feebly. He was cowering as he spoke.

"Please masters, we have nothin' left. You've taken everything. Please leave us alone!" The old mouse fell to his knees. Theodore turned to his friends.

"Obviously this fellow knows royalty when he sees it."

"I think he's scared out of his mind," Maggie said.

"Scared? Nonsense. What is there to be frightened of?" He turned to the old mouse kneeling before him. "Get up, my man. We mean you no harm." The old mouse raised his head.

"You…you're not sent by Toad?"

The three look quizzically at each other.

"No. We are on a quest. This is the good mouse, Jeremy. And this is Maggie, of Royal Pond, and I am King Theodore. But of course you know that."

A young girl mouse ran forward to help the old mouse to his feet. Maggie noticed Jeremy studying her very closely. Theodore continued.

"We're looking for some "Raccoon" persons. You haven't seen any have you? We were told we could find them in Dumptown. Which I assume this is, although I don't know about the 'town' part…"

"If they're here in Dumptown of their own free will, then they must work for Toad," said the girl mouse.

"This Toad fella, you don't happen to know where we could find him do ya'?" Maggie asked. The girl mouse set her feet defiantly.

"If you're friends o' Toad, you're not welcome here! Now go!"

"We didn't say we were friends of anybody," said Jeremy. "We just asked if you knew where to find him."

The girl, walked up toe to toe with Jeremy and placed her hands on her hips.

"Toad is a vile, cruel, swine, he is! He takes taxes from everyone in Dumptown. Makes the ones who can't pay work in his "City", he calls it. And then, if it's not bad enough already, his henchmen run all about the place takin' whatever else they want whenever they want it. So…" and her eyes got very squinty and angry, "if you're friends of Toad's, you're no friends of ours!"

Jeremy was speechless.

"We just wanna find these raccoons, okay?" Maggie said. "Take it easy, jeeze."

"Then, I wish you luck strangers," said the old mouse. "Toad is treacherous and powerful. He probably already knows you're here. I apologize for Erin. Toad took all that we had, even her mother's things. But…enough about Toad. You look tired and hungry. We don't have much, but you're welcome ta' stay the night and have supper with us."

"No really we wouldn't think of it we--," started Theodore.

"We'd be glad to," Jeremy said quickly.

"Then, welcome, lad." The old mouse threw an arm around Jeremy and the two walked off leaving Maggie and Theodore staring at Jeremy, bewildered.

That evening, Theodore sat on a small tin can. Another fly buzzed by and with a flick of the frog's tongue, it was captured and swallowed.

Maggie was pecking at a piece of watermelon rind. She held her broken wing out away from her body. Ice cream sticks formed the splint around her feathers.

Jeremy was being served one small bean and a bit of carrot by Erin. His eyes hadn't left her all day.

"I must say food is quite abundant here," Theodore said happily to Maggie as he whipped out his tongue for another fly.

"Maybe frog food. Not mouse food. This Toad

must be a real jerk."

Jeremy was in good spirits as he approached his friends and sat down next to Maggie.

"How's your wing?" he asked Maggie.

"Okay, long as I don't think of it as a wing."

"I had an uncle who once broke his leg, " Theodore said absently, "Never could plan on which way he'd hop." He caught another fly.

Jeremy stood up.

"I think I should talk to the girl alone and uhm...see if I can get any more information about this place," He didn't wait for their reply. He simply walked away with a spring in his step.

"Cupid makes ya' stupid," Maggie said as she watched him go.

"What?" asked Theodore.

"Jeremy. Nothin' can make ya' act dopier than love."

"You mean Jeremy and this...this...really?"

"Yup."

"Hmm. Never had the pleasure, myself. No time, you see. And I'd have to marry a princess. And most princesses are quite difficult to deal with." Then he frowned. "At least she's not a cabaret singer." 'ZIP', Theodore's tongue shot out and reeled in another fly.

At the far end of the mouse village, Erin was washing clothes in a bottle cap tub. Jeremy strolled over, watching her go about her chore.

"Sorry things are so bad here."

Erin wiped her brow.

"If I were braver," Erin said, rubbing clothes against the rough bottle cap rim, "it might not be so bad."

"I think you're really brave."

"You do?" she said, wiping a soapy arm across her forehead.

Jeremy nodded. She smiled.

"Toad took everything we had. Cups, saucers, my mother's harp, her wedding dress. Everything but her necklace, see?" She held it out. "Isn't it the most beautiful thing you've ever laid your eyes on?" Jeremy smiled and nodded again.

"You must be brave to be on such a quest."

"Nope. Usually I run when it gets dangerous," Jeremy admitted.

"I'd say that was the wisest course, most of the time," she replied, not looking up.

"I don't think it has anything to do with wisdom," admitted Jeremy. "More like just being afraid." He shook his head. He couldn't figure out why he was being so honest. He wasn't even this honest with himself.

"Look," said Erin, "any fool can find trouble if he's a mind to. Takes a brave mouse to admit tah' bein' afraid. Too many braggarts and blowhards in this world as it is, believe me."

Jeremy couldn't take his eyes off her. It seemed somehow that he'd known her for a very long time. Or that, in a very short time, she knew him.

"Hey, Erin," Jeremy began and moved close, next to her, "...do you think...I know we only met a little while ago, but do you think it's possible to..."

"I think…" Erin said as she touched her nose to his, "that it's time you should go back with you friends and get some rest. Don't you?"

Erin's eyebrows rose up as if the question was not really a question.

"Oh. Oh sure," Jeremy replied, a little confused and left her to her work.

Erin watched him as he walked away. He was disappointed, she could tell. And she noticed that she was smiling. She shook off the smile, glancing up at the moon which was rising slowly over a hill of rusting junk and smiled. The moon was almost full.

CHAPTER NINETEEN

The same moon glimmered across the pond through Gypsy's dressing room window. The noise from the main room of the cabaret filtered up through the floor of her room as she got ready for the next show. In the middle of the floor of Gypsy's room stood Archibald Rivvit, looking at himself in a full-length mirror. He was dressed in black tails, a gold rimmed monocle, and a red sash across his chest.

Two webbed hands appeared around his neck and adjusted his bow tie. Archibald turned around with a suave expression and kissed Gypsy's hand. This thrilled her beyond measure. It was a gesture of the upper classes. A ladder that Gypsy had spent a lifetime trying to find, let alone climb.

"Oh, Archie, you look so handsome."

"I can't help it my dear," he replied, a little bored. "I was born that way."

"So tell me again, Archie," she said, kissing him on the cheek, "when do I get to be a real lady? In the Palace and everything?"

"In due time, my dear, in due time. First, the necklace. Then the Coronation. Then...well, other things."

"But what if they don't find the necklace, love?"

"No matter. It doesn't work anyway. The power of the necklace is merely an old fable. Its the principle of the thing. The symbol of my destiny. No one will dispute my being King if I have the necklace."

"But what happens if the moles bring it back and it doesn't work? Won't they be mad?"

"You must remember we're dealing with primitive minds, m'dear. It takes all the mental powers the moles can muster just to put one foot in front of the other. I'll simply tell them that they dropped it, which undoubtedly they will have done along the way, and that it's broken—useless."

Gypsy snuggled up closer.

"You have such a clever mind, Archie."

Archibald's eyebrows darted up and down and he leered at her.

"Frightening, isn't it? By the way, did I ever tell you, you have the most gorgeous legs on Royal Pond?"

Gypsy batted her big eyelashes and giggled.

"Oh Archie," she said, "you're so romantic."

CHAPTER TWENTY

The whole mouse village was turned out to see Jeremy, Theodore, and Maggie off the next morning. The old mouse was there, too.

"Good journey to you," said the old mouse. "May your days be good ones and may the wind be at your back. Best if the wind's at your back around here. Dumptown isn't exactly a bed of roses, ya' know."

"It would help if they had a guide, father," came a voice from behind. They turned to see Erin standing there, dressed for travel, with a pack slung over her shoulder. "They'll never find their way to Toad otherwise," she said.

The old mouse started to sputter. "Now… now… don't you even be thinkin' about that, girl!".

"And why not?"

"Why not! Why not! Have ya' lost your mind entirely!"

"He's right," Jeremy said quickly, "It's too dangerous for a girl."

Erin faced Jeremy. Her eyes became fierce.

"Its me, or no one! Or you'll wander around this dump till you drop, or till Toad's patrol finds ya'!"

"I think we should take her," Maggie piped in. "And come to think of it, I'm a "girl" too."

"Well...one's enough!" Jeremy snapped back.

Erin turned to Theodore for the last word. She crossed her arms. He wasn't concerned at all.

"Of course you may be our guide, my dear," Theodore said as he motioned for Jeremy. Jeremy stepped close and Theodore whispered in his ear. "She wants to follow me, dear boy. It's quite normal. The peasant classes can't help it, you see."

Jeremy threw up his hands in hopeless disgust and stomped away.

"The full moon is only a day or two away and my cousin will be crowned King," Theodore announced to all present. "So, "tah", all. I'm sure it was a pleasure meeting me, but all good things must come to an end." Theodore then turned and started hopping down the path away from the village.

Maggie leaned next to Erin. "Don't worry, he grows on ya' after a while."

CHAPTER TWENTY ONE

By mid-day, Erin was in the lead as they rounded a large pile of old tires. Jeremy was bring up the rear, grumbling. Theodore rode on Maggie's back as she waddled along.

"You doing okay, your Highness?" Maggie asked. Theodore was perspiring and looked very pale.

"I...don't believe...(gasp)...I've ever been this long without water."

"There's a stream that runs just up ahead," Erin said. "Passed that big thing." The 'big thing' she pointed to was a huge rusted truck that sat in a cemetery of discarded tires. Erin let Maggie pass her while she waited for Jeremy to catch up.

"You haven't spoken a word since we left my village," she said to Jeremy, giving him a smile.

"Why should I? You've got everything under control. I mean, it's not like they need me or anything. They'd probably be better off without me. Besides, now even a girl can show me up. Perfect!"

"Show you up? Me? What's wrong with you? I thought you'd be glad I came? I thought cha'... well I thought... ugh! Never mind! I thought you at least cared about THOSE two? I thought you were on an important QUEST." She gazed at him for a long time.

"Maybe you were right, Jeremy. Maybe you ARE a coward after all. Because cowards only think about one thing. Themselves."

She started to walk away, then turned.

"I'm sorry I came. I thought there was more to you than just the way things look. I thought you had loyalty and honor. They're not your friends at all, are they? Not really. The truth is, you're using them for some stupid reason of your own. Well... your friends deserve better." Saying no more, she ran off to catch up to Maggie and Theodore.

Jeremy yelled after her, "They ARE my friends!" But after he said it, he felt ashamed.

CHAPTER TWENTY TWO

As Maggie, Theodore, and Erin rounded a tall stack of steel drums, they came upon a small stream lined with clumps of grass and trash. Theodore and Maggie made a dash for the water. When Maggie reached the edge of the stream she stopped suddenly, sending Theodore flying off her back and into the water.

"Whoa!" Theodore yelled as he flew through the air and hit the water with a splash.

The sun was reflecting on the water so that Maggie and Erin couldn't see beneath the surface. They waited, and waited, but Theodore never came up. Maggie started to worry and stepped into the stream, bending her head low to peer into the water. When her head was almost touching the water, a green shape came flying out and landed with a "squish" on the bank. It was Theodore.

"Is that what it's like to fly!" he said as he hopped up and down. "How WONDERFUL!" he said, and dove back into the water. Maggie and Erin both laughed.

"See?" said Maggie, "I told ya'. He kind o' grows on ya'."

Erin had found some shade under a tire, but Jeremy kept his distance. He knew she'd been right. He just couldn't think of a way to apologize now.

Now she knew he was a coward. There was no changing that. Not ever.

He walked up to Erin as if nothing had happened.

"I think I'm gonna scout around," he said, waiting for her to tell him not to. Waiting for some way say he was sorry.

"Makes no difference to me," she said, looking off.

"Well...fine then," he said, more embarrassed than ever.

Theodore was on Maggie's back again as they came out of the stream.

"Help me down from here, good mouse," he called to Jeremy. "I need a bit of supper, I think."

Jeremy was angry. He was angry at himself, but his anger wasn't a tiny focused beam of light, it was like a blowtorch that wanted to burn anything it could touch.

"I'm not your 'good mouse', and I'm not your 'servant', okay!" Jeremy shouted. "No wonder they don't want you back at Royal Pond! You can't do a thing by yourself! Everybody's just a servant to you! Because of you, the Pond is gonna have a terrible King, and everybody's gonna suffer! But you don't care about anything except getting supper on time and keeping your stupid feet wet!"

Jeremy spun on his heels, leaving Theodore

stunned. As he walked off, Erin tried her best not to look up. When she finally did, he was out of sight. Theodore was still sitting astride Maggie's back. He was very quiet.

CHAPTER TWENTY THREE

For almost an hour, Jeremy wandered through the dump feeling terrible about what he had said to Theodore. He knew he was just as bad as Theodore, in his own way. All he cared about was proving he wasn't a coward. He cared about that more than his friends, more than the quest, more than Royal Pond, more than anything. Erin was right, he wasn't brave at all. He'd never cared about anything enough to BE brave. And now he'd probably lost the best friends he'd ever had.

He was standing in front of a towering pile of wood and dead leaves when his round little ears began to pick up scuffling noises coming from nearby. He looked up just as a torrent of leaves and tiny sticks came flying at him from the center of the pile. He jumped for cover under an old cereal box just as a head popped out of the pile of sticks and leaves.

It was Winkie.

Winkie came tumbling down the pile of leaves along with clinking cans and clunking bottles. At the bottom of the pile he sat spitting and brushing leaves away from his eyes. His eye twitched madly as it became accustomed to the light of day. More leaves flew out of the pile and Danny came tumbling down, then Slick. Fatbottom finally poked his head out of the hole at the top of the pile and yawned lazily.

Jeremy adjusted his position under the cereal box. The cereal box was held up by an even smaller matchbox. Jeremy leaned forward in order to get a better view.

Fatbottom couldn't seem to squeeze himself out of the pile, so Winkie, Danny, and Slick climbed back up the pile, grabbed his arms, and started pulling. It was not an easy task since, like an iceberg, Fatbottom's biggest part was always underneath him.

With one big yank by all three, Fatbottom came hurtling out of the hole. They all went somersaulting down to the bottom of the pile where Fatbottom landed atop them all with a "CHRUNCH!".

"Uugh!" Winkie muttered, "I think my buh-buh-buh-back's broken!"

"Get off!" Danny grunted, "I can't breath!"

Fatbottom rolled off of them and crawled to his feet. Winkie, twitching more than ever, scrambled to his feet and stepped with his right front paw on an old spatula. The spatula handle flipped up and whacked him in the nose and he fell backward into the trash again.

Danny staggered to his feet and noticed that Slick was still lying face down, smooshed in the damp earth, motionless.

"Hey mates! We flattened Slick!"

They peeled Slick off the ground and turned him over. His eyes were crossed and his tongue was hanging out.

"Strike him on the back, comrades!" Fatbottom shouted.

They turned Slick over and they all started beating him on the back, his eyes bugging out and his tongue unraveling like a party favor with every blow. Finally he started to cough and they backed away.

"You were flat as a p-p-pancake, mate" Winkie said to Slick.

"I thought you was 'done in' old boy," Fatbottom said.

"He's alright," Danny said, "Come on, let's get out of this dump."

They start walking away when Slick teetered and fell flat on his face again.

At that same instant, Jeremy's weight made the matchbox holding up the cereal box give way. The heavy cereal box fell, hitting Jeremy on the head, trapping him underneath.

The movement of the box made the raccoons forget about Slick. As Fatbottom lifted the cereal box up, they saw Jeremy lying there on the ground. Jeremy's head was spinning so much, he didn't notice as he was lifted up by the tail. Fatbottom inspected him closely.

"There are spies everywhere," Fatbottom said.

Jeremy was so dizzy he was seeing six or seven raccoons in front of him. Danny shoved his nose against Jeremy's.

"You know what we do with spies don't ya'?" Danny said.

"Yeah, don't ya'?" Winkie asked.

Jeremy was quivering.

"I-I'm n-n-not a spy," Jeremy said, his eyes crossing and uncrossing.

Slick finally got up from the ground. He was still hallucinating, and saw Jeremy flapping his arms, trying to escape. Delirious, Slick thought Jeremy was a butterfly.

"A butterfly," Slick said, staggering forward. "A pretty little butterfly." Slick grabbed Jeremy from Fatbottom and tossed him into the air.

"Fly! Be free!"

"Ahhh!!" Jeremy screamed.

"Don't ya' luv them li'oh things?" Slick said to no one in particular.

Winkie grabbed Slick by the neck with one hand and started slapping him with the other.

"S-s-s-snap out of it!" Winkie said, and let Slick fall down face first first.

Meanwhile, Fatbottom dove for Jeremy and

caught him just before he hit the ground. Winkie and Danny sighed in relief.

Slick got to his feet, his head spinning, then suddenly remembered Winkie slapping him. He kicked Winkie from behind so hard it drove Winkie's pot belly up to his neck, then down again.

"Nobody slaps me! Ya' got that, bloke!" Slick said to Winkie.

"Alright," Winkie said, his hair standing on end, "it's l-l-l-lights out for you, mate!" The two raccoons lunged for each other.

"Hey! Hey! Stop it! We've got a spy to take care of here," said Danny.

"I'm not a spy!" Jeremy yelled.

"That's what they ALL say. If your not a spy, then who are you?" asked Danny.

"Nobody..." Jeremy began. At which point Fatbottom started shaking him by the tail.

"I'm...I'm looking for a necklace!" Jeremy shouted. The shaking stopped. He'd finally said something that got their attention.

"Necklace? What necklace?" Danny asked suspiciously.

"A silver one," Jeremy said.

"With a guh-guh-guh-green, sparkly in it?" Winkie asked.

"I've come to take it back to its rightful owner, okay?"

"So you're going to take it away from Toad, are ya'? All by your teeny weeny little self?" Danny asked.

"Where'd the butterfly go?" Slick said, still not quite himself.

"I vote for mouse fondue, forth with" said Fatbottom with hungry eyes.

"Wait!" Danny said. He turned to Jeremy, "What makes you think you can get this necklace back?"

"I have friends," Jeremy said.

This really got the raccoon's attention. They looked around nervously.

" Ah, he's luh-luh-lyin'," Winkie said.

"I say, Mouse flambe," said Fatbottom said, licking his lips.

"Wait a minute, boys! Wait a minute! Let me think..." said Danny, and he began to pace back and forth while everyone waited patiently. Jeremy's eyes were getting redder and redder from hanging upside down. He tried his best to kick at Fatbottom's fingers, but it was useless and his head pounded even harder. Finally Danny stopped and looked as if someone had turned on a light somewhere inside his head.

"Why not?" Danny said.

"What?" Slick asked.

"Toad's been quite rude to us, after all the

trouble we went through to bring him what he wanted. I was rather disappointed by his behavior. He just might need to be taken down a peg or two."

"Hmmm ..." whispered Fatbottom, posing a finger in the air, "Prompted to my revenge by Heaven or--."

"You mean g-g-g-get back at Toad?" Winkie asked. "And that s-s-s-slithering snake in the grass?"

"And those flyin' rats?" offered Slick.

Danny took Jeremy from Fatbottom, still holding him by the tail.

"Alright runt. We might be able ta' help you out."

Jeremy was furious by now, and was spun back and forth trying to get free. "Then let me down!"

Danny dropped him into a clump of grass. When he got up he was pink with anger. "Help me out?" he asked. "How?"

"In finding that li'oh trinket you was talkin' about," Slick said.

Jeremy stood still. "You know where it is?"

They all nodded.

"Well then, first I have to get my friends."

"Just lead the way, runt," Danny said.

"My name is JEREMY."

"Right," said Danny, "anything you say, runt...."

CHAPTER TWENTY FOUR

Jeremy and the raccoons rounded the edge of the pile of tires where he had left Theodore, Maggie, and Erin. Jeremy was shocked to find the area empty.

"They wouldn't leave without me. I know they wouldn't. They were right here!"

"Maybe they got scared and took off," suggested Slick.

"No! They wouldn't do that!"

"Well then," Danny said, rubbing his gray furry chin and looking around at the others, "that leaves only one other explanation."

Jeremy saw Erin's necklace on the ground and ran over to pick it up. He held it in the air. Danny nodded.

"Toad."

CHAPTER TWENTY FIVE

Theodore and Erin were standing before Toad's statue-throne with two rats behind them holding fountain pen spears at their backs. Pierre was within striking distance, just in case. The snake was winding his way round and round the base of the fountain, which was his way of pacing back and forth. Maggie struggled against four snickering rats who had her confined underneath an old fish net.

Toad sat in the statue's marble hands atop the fountain and addressed his captives.

"I've long been a believer in fate. And this, more or less proves I'm right. I mean, here I am, about to complete my life's work, work for which I was banished from Royal Pond, and who should show up but their present King. Must be a sign, don't you think?" Toad smiled at Theodore. "All's well that ends well, eh?" He swept the room with his hand.

"How do you like my little summer home?"

Erin couldn't restrain herself any longer.

"Have you no respect for royalty! Ya' traitor, ya'!!"

Toad laughed in deep croaks and raised his arms up in the air. Pilar fluttered down and grabbed his hands. Gently, she lifted him over the edge of the fountain, and lowered his jelly-like body to the ground.

Toad waddled forward toward Erin and, with a finger, stroked underneath her soft furry chin.

"A pretty little thing, don't you think, Pierre?" Erin struggled and Pierre laughed in short hisses as his face came within inches of Erin's.

"Too bad you chose your friends so unwisely," said Toad. "Still...I believe I shall be kind and turn you into something pretty. A flower, perhaps." He turned to Maggie, who was bent over from the weight of the net on top of her.

"And you, Duck, something a bit more creative... something between a snail and a lizard, perhaps." Maggie lunged for Toad, but the net snapped her back to the ground.

Toad, at last, approached Theodore.

"But you, my distant cousin—you will be my masterpiece. My wildest imagination put to the test. I will turn you into the most hideous--disgusting--miserable creature the world has ever known."

"Uhm...not to be negative, but, precisely HOW do you intend to do all of this...'turning into' rot?" Theodore asked, still holding his head high.

"The Royal Necklace of course," said Toad.

Theodore began to chuckle. "Really? Well, good luck with that. The necklace has no power. It's all a stupid legend."

Toad put his face against Theodore's so that they were eyeball to eyeball.

"So they all thought... your small-minded ancestors. They feared my genius and banished me from the pond! Sent me out to die! They couldn't imagine that the power of the necklace could actually be REAL, that all the legends were true, and that I could restore its power!"

"What power?"

"The power you will be the first to experience, "Sire"! More power than you can imagine, "Your Majesty, Your "Highness!""

Toad motioned and Pilar fluttered down again, lifting him up and placing him on a platform suspended over the large metal transformer. The thick electric cables seemed to grow out of each side of the metal transformer, curling around to hang over the sides of the platform. The ends of both cables gleamed from the bright exposed copper wire hooks.

Toad proclaimed in a loud voice, "Very shortly, the Royal Necklace will be attached to these copper hooks. A tremendous flow of electricity--artificial lightning, if you will--will travel through these cables and strike the medallion." Toad spread his arms wide, raised his head, and closed his eyes. "Then, the power of the necklace will be restored! And I, TOAD, shall achieve my destiny!" Toad lost his victorious grin when he heard laughter.

It was Theodore.

"You're batty as a loon!" Theodore said with a chuckle.

"What?" said Toad, thrown that someone would dare laugh at him.

"Well...you can't honestly believe that rubbish? Even if you could somehow charge the ruddy thing, you're not of the royal bloodline. According to the legend, only those with yellow eyes can use the power of the neck--"

"Ahh!" Toad roared with rage! "YES! You'd like me to believe that, wouldn't you! Your ancestors told me the same thing! So, I did experiments on children and proved it!"

"Really?" asked Theodore, not convinced.

"Well… alright! Didn't go exactly as planned back then, but the children DID change! Just into hideously awful slimy things! But that's not the point, is it! It proved I was right! The power COULD be restored!" Toad began to waddle back and forth, his body quivering like jelly. "But would they listen? No! All because a hundred or so children go missing I'm some kind of villain? Genius requires SACRIFICE! How dare they banish me! TOAD!"

He waddled forward face to face with Theodore. "I'll have my revenge! And when I return to Royal Pond, I'll destroy every living creature on it!" At that point, Toad began gasping for air and had to lean back against a wooden post on the platform. Pilar flew down and fanned him with her wing. Soon he regained his composure.

"Pierre? Show our guests to their room, won't you. They begin to bore me."

Pierre led the way and the six rats dragged their three prisoners over to a chicken wire cage that sat in shadows cast by the hanging Christmas lights in the rafters. The rats shoved the captives inside the cage and closed the door. Pierre inserted a nail in the latch, flicked his tongue at them a few times, and slithered away.

"Could it be true, then?" Erin asked Theodore.

"Don't see how," Theodore answered. "But then, Toad was believed to be a genius."

"Either way we're in deep trouble," Maggie muttered.

Theodore looked suddenly very depressed. He squatted down on his spring-like legs and buried his head in his hands.

"All my life I thought it was all just a silly game. The Necklace, the ceremonies, all the traditions. If Toad's right, if the legends ARE true, I've been a fool. Jeremy was right. Let's face it, chaps, I don't know what it's like to be a good King. Never cared about anyone else but myself. When I think of how my people will suffer under my Cousin Archie....or worse yet, Toad..." he shivered. "They needed me and I failed them...and now look what I've done to both of you..." Theodore sighed and slumped his shoulders so that his fingers touched the floor.

They waited in silence for what seemed like hours. The sounds of Toad's city rumbled on. It might have been day or night, it was hard to tell. But they didn't speak. They were each lost in their own thoughts.

Just then, the ground beneath them began to shake and bounce. The wire cage rattled violently and along with it came an odd clawing sound. With a "POP!", a head burst out of the earth within the cage floor. Then, with another "POP!", another head emerged.

It was Charlie and Irving.

They shook their heads, spitting and sputtering at the taste of dirt in their mouths.

"Where are we?" Charlie asked, squinting in the dim light.

"I don't know," answered Irving. "YOU had the map."

"What?"

"The secret map," Irving repeated.

"Oh, 'dat map," said Charlie, looking a little puzzled.

"So...where is it?" Irving asked.

""I must o' forgot it, I guess," Charlie answered. Irving was furious.

"You blockhead! How could you forget the secret map?"

"It's a secret map, alright! You gotta hide it in a secret place. I just forgot where I hid it."

"Mom always said there was somethin' wrong wit' you," Irving grumbled. "I should o'--" For the first time the two moles, heads sticking out of the dirt, noticed the wire cage around them.

They squeezed their upper bodies out of the holes and looked around. Then Charlie shoved Irving with both hands.

"You took us right ta' JAIL! You dummy!"

"You were the one in front!" Irving said and pushed Charlie back, which led to a wrestling match with their lower bodies still lodged in the dirt. They tussled and punched, and grunted until a voice caught their limited attention.

"I say, chaps?" Theodore called to them. The moles stopped and looked around. The voice came from a frog sitting with his arms tied in front of him. They glanced at each other, then back at the frog.

"You wouldn't mind undoing these bonds, would you?" Theodore said, holding out his arms bound in string. "They chafe something awful."

The moles shot each another glance and then shook their heads in a definite "No."

"Not a chance," said Irving.

"No way, Green Boy," said Charlie. "We don't have time. We gotta get the necklace back."

"Yeah," added Irving, "we untie you and pretty soon everybody'll be askin' us to untie 'em, and then..." Irving suddenly slapped a paw to his forehead. "Just great!" he said, shoving Charlie again, "First you lose our secret map, now you give away our secret plans about stealin' the necklace back!"

Charlie clamped a hand over his own mouth as if to stop the tide of stupidity from tumbling out. It was an impossible task, of course.

"But we're here for the necklace too," Erin said getting to her feet. She smiled sweetly.

The moles looked at Erin as Erin fluttered her eyes at them. The two moles sucked in their stomachs, stuck out their chests, and tried to slick down the spiky fur on the tops of their heads. Irving gave a little wave.

"We could do it together!" Maggie offered.

"We might even make... another secret plan," Theodore said in a low secretive way.

At that, both moles forgot about Erin and looked at Theodore with great interest.

"How secret?" Irving asked.

"I can't tell you that, now can I?" Theodore said. "Then it wouldn't be a secret."

Charlie and Irving thought it over. "He's smart,

'dis guy," Charlie said.

"But you have to untie us first," Theodore reminded them.

The moles looked at each other, then spoke in unison. "Deal!"

CHAPTER TWENTY SIX

Jeremy and the four Raccoons arrived in Toad City by late afternoon. By the time they led Jeremy to the rear of a large wooden shack it was night. Jeremy looked up and noticed the moon was up and almost full.

"Toad calls this 'Toad City'," said Danny. "If your friends are alive, they'll be inside here."

"It used to be an old shack," Slick said. "There's a loose board around here somewhere," he said, and began inspecting the boards that made up the wall. They all started pulling at the boards, trying to find an entrance to the shack. Jeremy found a board that gave a bit but it was too much for him.

"Hey fellas," he said, "how about this one?" Jeremy strained at the board as Fatbottom reached over and gave it a yank.

The board smacked Jeremy in the face and he went flying.

"Whoa!" said Slick, "Fatbottom, you don't know your own strength!" Fatbottom took a few body-builder poses while the other raccoons whispered "BRAVO! YAY! WHAT A BODY!"

Jeremy stomped back to them, rubbing his nose and fuming.

"Thanks a lot!" he said. "Could you guys be serious for one minute? We don't have time for this you know!"

Slick grabbed the loose board and pulled it back just enough to get Jeremy through. When he was inside, the board suddenly snapped back, sending the little rodent flying into the shack. Fatbottom, Winkie, and Danny all look at Slick. Slick shrugged and said, "Couldn't help myself." They all snickered.

Toad City was amazing. Groups of rats, mice, possums, bats, voles, and lizards busied themselves with their appointed duties. Colored lights ran the course of the ceiling and reminded Jeremy of colored stars. At one side of the City sat the enormous transformer, which was also decorated with strings of Christmas lights. The raccoons lined up behind Jeremy.

"Quite a show," Winkie said without a single stutter.

"Where would my friends be?" Jeremy asked.

"Phff...how should we know," Slick said.

"Let's split up, boys." said Danny. "And watch out for that snake."

The raccoons split off in different directions, and Jeremy melted into the crowd of Toad's workers.

CHAPTER TWENTY SEVEN

Inside Toad's dressing room, Toad stood draped in what looked like red velvet curtains. He looked like an ancient Roman, if the ancient Romans had been fat greenish toads.

The three bats were with him, hanging upside down in various parts of the room. Toad stretched out his arms and Hector flew down from his perch to adjust the velvet on Toad's body. Miguel placed a wreath of flowers on Toad's head, as Pilar covered Toad's face with powder and rouge. Toad looked at himself in the mirror.

"Oh, you look hot, baby!" Pilar said, and whistled as she fluttered a few feet away.

"Yeah boss," Hector said, "You look too good for this crowd, man."

"They should like, make a statue of you or something, you know?" Hector added.

"Thank you," Toad said, waving his hand as if it was a great effort. "Thank you all. Take a good look at the evil ruler you've come to love and adore. Today, after a lifetime of waiting, I shall gain a power beyond imagining!"

The bats all clapped their wings in applause.

A hiss came from one corner of the room. Through a small opening in the wall, came the rattlesnake, Pierre. Toad glanced at the snake's reflection in the mirror, and Pierre bowed, nearly folding himself in half. Hector backed away, out of striking distance.

"Why don't 'chu, climb back in your hole, slim," Hector said to the snake, "we got things covered here, okay?

Pierre hissed, showing his long fangs, and Hector bared his teeth too.

"You boys really should try to get along," Toad said as Pilar was curling his lashes, "You're like my family, you know," he said and seemed to be holding back tears. "The family I never had." He took out a hanky and blew his nose. "Of course, if you ever caused me any embarrassment I shouldn't think twice about killing you both."

Hector and Pierre both grimaced at the thought.

"Now, Pierre," Toad went on, "is everything ready?"

"Of course, my Commandant!" Pierre said in his hissy French accent. "My great leader! My idol!"

"Good. You've served me well, Pierre. And I do love the way you talk." Toad took a deep breath and clasped hands together. "It is time..." he said, and with Miguel and Pilar flitting out the door before him, Toad waddled out of the room,

"It's only because you are such a great guy, boss!" Pierre called after him. "I have a poster of you in my room!"

Hector made kissing noises, and Pierre spun around.

"Come eeer you leetle flying peep squeak!" Pierre hissed. "No, Meestair' Toadie to protect you now! Hah hah!"

Pierre waited for Hector, mouth open, fangs poised. Hector swooped around in circles, teasing the snake, and after a few near misses, made it passed him and out the door.

"Ha ha!" Hector jeered from the other side of the door, "Better cut down on the sweets, slim! You're getteen' slow man!"

Pierre sprang to the door, but Hector had already gone. He yelled at the bat, who was now a black dot in the distance.

"Come back here you leetle piece of flying doo doo!"

CHAPTER TWENTY EIGHT

As Toad appeared on the platform the crowd below began to cheer. He strutted over to the two copper hooks and the necklace, which was now stretched between them. He raised his hands and the crowd went silent.

"The hour has come! This day will go down in history as a new beginning! The start of a new age! Soon Dumptown and its residents will be the envy of creatures all over the earth!"

The crowd began to chant "Toad", "Toad", over and over. Some of Toad's henchmen, were passing out banners that had "Toad" printed on them. Jeremy squeezed his way through the chanting mass until he reached the second row. With a grandiose gesture, Toad stretched one arm into the air. The chanting stopped.

"Ready the switch!" he bellowed.

To the side of the platform, a lizard grabbed a slender piece of twine that attached to the red handle of an electrical switchbox. It tied the other end of the twine onto a net bag filled with rocks.

"Behold! My power!" Toad shouted and with a swift motion, brought his arm down.

Two possums pushed the net bag of rocks over the edge of the wooden platform. As the net fell, the twine jerked the switch down with a "Thwack!"

Electricity bulged through the cables and within moments two rivers of current reached the slender silver chain of the necklace and struck it like a thunderbolt. One by one the silver links of the chain accepted the power until it reached the medallion. A torrent of sounds, voices, and music filled the air as the artificial lightning was absorbed into the medallion. Then, the building filled with a ball of brilliant green light and animals were squinting or turning away. Even Toad was forced to cover his eyes. There was a roar of sound that went on for at least a minute and rattled the boards of the shack itself.

"Enough!" Toad yelled. "Turn it off!"

The lizard scrambled up the post and placed another piece of twine on the same switch. The possums, already waiting on a higher platform pushed another net of rocks over the edge and as the twine became taut, the switch was yanked upward again.

There was a "FOOP!" as sound and light were seemed to be sucked out of the shack.

Toad walked up to the glowing necklace, almost afraid to touch it. His fingers caressed the warm chain. He reverently pulled the necklace off the hook and placed it about his neck. Jeremy's mouth was hanging open, as was the crowd around him. Toad leaned back and laughed insanely.

"Ha ha ha ha ha!! At last! Mine! Mi---"

"Stop!" came a voice from behind Toad. Toad turned, dumbfounded.

Behind him, feet apart in defiance, was Theodore. Theodore's arms were crossed and his lip was sticking out pompously. Toad's shock slowly turned into a grin.

"Just in time, your Majesty," Toad said.

"The necklace belongs to Royal Pond, you fiend!" Theodore shouted. "I command you to give it to me!"

Toad began to laugh and the crowd below joined in with laughter as well. Jeremy, in the midst of the crowd, was shocked and relieved to see Archibald. He looked around for Maggie and Erin but they were not to be seen. He weaved his through the crowd and disappeared.

"Give it to you?" Toad said. "Oh, very well. If that's what you want." Pilar was sneaking up behind Theodore. Her talons were outstretched as she got closer and closer. Toad continued.

"According to the legend, all I have to do is point..." Toad pointed his fat hand at Theodore and the necklace began to glow. The greenish glow flowed from the medallion and down Toad's arm, where it seemed to gather. Suddenly a bolt of green lightning shot out of Toad's arm straight at Theodore.

Theodore hopped into the air just as Pilar made a grab for him. With a "POOF" Pilar was struck by the green bolt of lightning.

As everyone watched in stunned silence, the bat's body began to change, twisting and writhing on the ground. Smoke rose from her body as Miguel came diving down from the rafters to help her.

"I'll save you, Pilar!" he yelled.

With a "POP" Pilar's new form was complete. There in her place was a creature with feathers, three feet, some crooked teeth, and an eye in the middle of her forehead. Miguel flapped to a screeching halt.

"Whoa! You've changed, woman! You look like... like the creature of the bat lagoon!"

Toad roared with anger, took aim, and fired again.

Theodore hopped into the air once more and this time the bolt struck the lizard on the platform. The lizard turned it into a slimy toothless blob with eight feet. Theodore jumped off of the platform and into the crowd. The crowd went wild, scattering in all directions.

Toad began unleashing bolts of green lightning at random now. Lizards, mice, rats, possums were being zapped, one after the other, as Theodore kept hopping out of Toad's aim.

Miguel dove down at Theodore, but kept missing. As Theodore neared an old fire extinguisher, the bat swooped once more. At that moment, Erin popped out of the fire extinguisher nozzle and and threw a metal washer like a Frisbee at Miguel, hitting him squarely on the head. The throw made her lose her balance, and out of the nozzle she went. As the bat tumbled to the ground, so did Erin.

Jeremy caught sight of Erin for the first time. "Erin!" Jeremy screamed. He shoved his way through the panicked crowd, running for Erin. Meanwhile, Toad was sending green shafts of lightning, rapid fire, at Theodore.

"You can't escape, Rivvit!" Toad roared. "Stand still and take it like a Toad. Die!"

Theodore hopped, as a green bolt hit a piece of tin behind him. The blast ricocheted off the tin and hit a possum hiding inside a wooden crate. The possum's tail and hind quarters mushroomed into something reptilian and striped.

Pierre was off in a corner, waiting in the dark. He wasn't eager to become a striped bird crossed with an alligator, or a bug crossed with a fish, or a brainless glob of feathery goo. So he had decided to hide until Toad got hold of himself. But when he spotted Erin falling from the nozzle of the fire extinguisher, the temptation overpowered his own safety, and out he came.

Jeremy reached Erin, but she was unconscious. He lifted her to him. A moment later she opened her eyes and looked up at him. Drowsily she said, "You're not gonna blame all this on...me bein' a girl, are ya'?"

Jeremy hugged her just as he noticed a shadow rising over them. He turned to see Pierre poised and ready to strike. Jeremy shoved Erin aside and jumped just as Pierre lunged. Pierre's fangs sank into the dirt floor. There was a round white tack on the floor in front of Jeremy. As Pierre was spitting dirt out of his mouth, Jeremy picked up the tack and threw it Frisbee-style at the reptile. The tack stuck in Pierre's nose. Pierre went cross-eyed, wrinkled his nose and shook it off.

"Now you have made Pierre angry! You leetle fur ball!" hissed the French snake.

Jeremy was gripped with terror. Pierre's eyes seem to glow red. He struck again, then again, and each time he barely missed the mouse. Jeremy took off in a panic.

When he reached a wooden crate hey ducked inside and peeked out. What he saw made his heart sink. Pierre was coiled up, staring down at Erin. Pierre's head was raised and his fangs were dripping poison. Erin was struggling to get to her feet, but kept falling back to the ground, dizzy from her fall.

Jeremy's couldn't get his feet to move. He looked at his tail, rigid and quivering. Alice had been right all along. He was a coward. And this time it would cost Erin her life.

Erin finally got to her feet and stood wobbling, facing the poisonous serpent. She stared at the snake, gritting her teeth at him as if daring the snake to strike her. Instead, Pierre whipped his tail around her small body, wrapping himself round and round, preparing to squeeze her to death.

Erin felt herself being crushed as Pierre's coils tightened around her. Her head was free, but was about to be covered by another loop of the snake's body. She tried to wriggle free, but she was no match for the strength of the snake. Her breath was slowly being squeezed out of her. "Quick," she thought, "let it be over quickly."

Then, unexpectedly, the coils loosened. She took a deep gasp of air and wriggled herself up through the middle of the coils. As her head cleared the top coil, she saw something amazing.

Jeremy was standing a few feet in front of Pierre holding a long rusted nail in both hands, like a sword. And the voice that came out of the tiny mouse didn't sound like Jeremy at all. It sounded angry and sure. It sounded brave.

"Let her go, you overgrown WORM! "

Pierre stiffened and reared his head at this. His

snake eyes narrowed into hateful slits. Steam hissed out of his nostrils. His head rose higher and higher.

"What do you say!! What am I 'eering!! No one calls me, the 'andsome Pierre, a WORM!!!"

Pierre struck.

Jeremy ducked and struck the snake with the nail. Pierre was so angry he completely forgot about Erin. He uncoiled and sprang at Jeremy again.

Next to Toad's statue-throne, dirt sprayed up through the soil. Charlie and Irving shook the dirt from their heads. They were wearing strips of orange caution flags around their heads. They looked like Japanese zeroes.

"Bonsai!" yelled Charlie.

"Bonsai!" shouted Irving.

They dove back into their holes and began digging around the base of the fountain. Round and round they dug. The fountain began to wobble, then teeter back and forth. With a "CRASH!" it struck the ground. Some of the Christmas lights attached to it were crushed, wires stretched and with a "TWANG!" snapped apart, sputtered, and sent sparks cascading into the air.

Toad heard the sound of the fallen statue and turned in horror to see his throne lying in ruins. He was insane with fury now. He whipped his fat body around looking for Theodore. He wasn't about to let a puny King of Royal Pond destroy his plans this time. Never!

"GET THAT BLASTED FROG!" he roared.

Two rats launched themselves at Theodore. The frog hopped high in the air and the rats crashed into each other. Theodore laughed triumphantly while still in mid-air, but he was cut short by a hand that grabbed him around the throat. A possum held him in its fist and showed his dirty teeth.

"Well, lookie hare'. I got me a frog. I hear'd frogs was mighty good eatin'. Mighty good."

Theodore's eyes bulged wider and wider as the possum squeezed. The possum's grin got toothier and toothier. "Yes sir, I jest luv' tuh' SQUEEZE thangs."

All of a sudden, a big club appeared from out of nowhere and bashed the possum on top of the head with a "BOINK". The possum's hand opened, and another hand grabbed Theodore. Slick was leaning out around the corner, Theodore in his hand. He looked at the possum, collapsed on the floor.

"And I jest luv' tuh' BASH things, mate," Slick said. A bolt of green lightening struck the post beside Slick. Both he and Theodore fell backwards onto a pile of empty paint cans.

Danny and Fatbottom ran over to help Slick,

and then all three started tossing paint cans, looking for Theodore. They found him inside one of the cans. Theodore looked up shyly at the Raccoons.

"...Hello chaps," Theodore said, thinking they were Toads henchmen, "I suppose the game up."

"Not hardly," Danny said, grinning.

"We're the reinforcements, you might say," Slick said, his shifty eyebrows moving up and down.

Just then, several rats jumped out at the raccoons. They all went down in a jumble of empty paint cans. Theodore made three great leaps and landed on top of the pile.

Toad City was in chaos.

Lizards, mice, possums, rats, weasels were running helter-skelter, trying to find cover from the green lightning bolts that were bouncing off the walls. No one was safe from the lightning bouncing around.

Toad was planted at the base of the pile of paint cans. He pointed his arm and sent a green bolt of lightning in a wide arc over the entire pile of cans hoping to hit the raccoons and Theodore all at the same time.

Danny, Fatbottom, Slick and Theodore all dove into the pile of cans and disappeared as if the cans were bubbles in a bubble bath. The rats that were attacking them looked around just in time to see the green bolt headed for them.

"Yipes!" said one of the rats just as the bolt struck them all. "ZAP!" and in a puff of smoke, the rats became bizarre creatures, one with a horn on its nose, another with an elephant-like trunk, and the other with a huge toothy mouth twice as big as it's crabby body. The force of the green blast sent the paint cans behind it spewing every which way.

Theodore was now rolling down the pile inside one of the cans. The can kept rolling and rolling down the pile heading straight for Toad. Toad's fat body couldn't get out of the way fast enough and with a "WHAM!" the can bowled him over.

Theodore rolled right over Toad, still inside the can, unable to stop until the can hit a tilted pot-bellied stove at the opposite end of Toad City.

Jeremy was in the middle of the floor fighting for his life. He thrust and parried as the Rattlesnake struck over and over with its vicious fangs. The rattles on Pierre's tail sounded like the drums of a marching army.

"Wait unteel I sink my fangs eento you, you leetle pain een zee neck!" Pierre hissed.

Erin struggled to her feet, watching the deathly duel as Jeremy jabbed and swung his rusty nail, dodging the fangs over and over. The rattlesnake was ten times his size, but, Jeremy kept fighting. He was like a knight doing battle with a fire-breathing dragon. Erin was mystified.

"Never," she whispered to herself, watching Jeremy do battle with the deadly snake, "I'll never see anything like it. Not if I live forever..."

From the shadows where they had taken cover, hundreds of eyes were watching Jeremy and Pierre fight. They were amazed. They had never seen any creature, no matter how big, who didn't run from at the sight of the rattlesnake. And now he was being kept at bay by a little gray mouse.

Pierre's long body and tail were stretched out across the floor. He didn't even bother to coil as he focused all his attention on Jeremy. Then he felt a tug on his tail. Erin had Pierre by the rattles of his tail and was pulling with all her might. Pierre whipped his tail around and sent Erin flying against the fallen fountain-throne. She slid to the ground and didn't move. Jeremy saw this and panicked. He dashed across the floor and stood in front of Erin, holding up the rusty nail, waiting for the snake.

Just then, from the darkness of the rafters, Hector swooped down behind Jeremy and scooped Erin up in his arms, carrying her into the air. Hector yelled down to Pierre.

"Hey Frenchie! Watch how a pro does it, baby!"

Both Pierre and Jeremy looked up as Hector

carried Erin higher and higher into the air. Pierre hissed at the bat, then turned back to Jeremy. Jeremy turned to face the snake slowly, all expression gone. He stared at the snake without blinking. It confused Pierre.

"I've wasted all the time I'm going to on you, snake," Jeremy said, again without any emotion. "Come on." This sounded so ridiculous Pierre began to laugh.

"Leeson to zee brave leetle mousy," he said as he began to slither forward. "I weel keel you, and zen, I weel keel your leetle mousy girlfriend up zair weeth zat stupid bat! Now... prepare to die."

Pierre's fangs sparkled as he drew back and lunged. Jeremy planted his feet firmly and swung the nail with all his might at the oncoming mouth.

As the nail made contact with Pierre's fangs, there was a loud "PING, PING" sound. Pierre suddenly jerked backwards. His lips were moving around strangely. Something was wrong. Hector called down from above.

"Hey, Frenchie! Kill that mouse, man! The party's over!"

The snake whipped around to face the bat and exposed his fangs. But he didn't have any fangs to expose. There on the ground before him, in front of that little grey mouse, lay his two long deadly fangs. Peirre began to whimper.

"Whoa!" Hector said in surprise. "Well, guess you won't have to worry about cavities anymore!"

While the snake was in shock, his rattled tail lay in front of Jeremy. The strand of Christmas tree lights was on the ground, some broken and sputtering sparks, some sockets empty. Jeremy picked up Pierre's tail and shoved hard it into one of the empty sockets.

There was a "SNAP" as electricity poured through Pierre's body, crackling and popping as it traveled up each inch of him. His body began to light up like a long narrow light bulb and his ribs were clearly visible through his scaly skin.

Jeremy turned and searched the rafters. He saw the bat, Erin in his arms, flying higher and higher. The bat was dodging bolts of green lightning.

Hector glanced up at an opening in the roof exposing the starry sky beyond. The battle was not going well. Time for him to find a safe cave somewhere. He looked down at Erin. She was just coming to. He and smiled as seductively as a bat could possibly smile and said, "Hey baby, how 'bout we go someplace an' get to know each other, you know? I mean, you're a rodent. I'm a rodent. Ju' know?" Erin didn't respond. "I mean, we wouldn't wanna have kids right away or notheen'. We could like, wait, and do some traveleen'. I could like, open a flight school..." He kept flapping his way to the opening in the roof. "Maybe we could move in with jore folks for a while..."

Huge dark wings appeared from the shadows. The sight of them pulled Hector up short. In mid air, Maggie lowered her face into the light.

"The only place you're movin' is down!" Maggie grabbed Erin with one foot and smashed the bat with her right wing. The bat flew across the shack, tumbling over and over until he went "SPLAT" against a plank on the far wall. Maggie looked down at Erin who was just waking up.

"Hope I didn't ruin a budding romance."

Toad finally got his enormously fat body to its feet.

The raccoons were still stumbling on the paint-can pile. Winkie had a can stuck on his head and was running back and forth crashing into things. Fatbottom, a can stuck on his opposite end was crawling with the can in the air and face in the dirt. Danny and Slick were clinging to each other just trying to stand up. Across floor, Theodore finally emerged from a pile of ashes inside the pot-bellied stove. He hopped to the floor, covered in gray soot. Toad spotted him.

"Now your Highness," Toad croaked, "this time no mistakes......"

Theodore closed his eyes awaiting his doom. Toad swelled up and took aim. A green glow began to fill Toad and rushed down his arm. Just as the glow reached his finger tips, Jeremy appeared out of nowhere, throwing himself at Toad. The mouse grabbed Toad's arm just as the lightning shot out of it and the bolt of lightning skittered off pipes and metal barrels, creating a kind of laser light show as the mouse and Toad wrestled each other on the dirt floor. Jeremy tried to pry Toad's arm back but the Toad was too strong and pushed Jeremy aside. Jeremy rolled away and stopped near some old drain pipes and rusted metal sinks.

Toad, panting, rose to his feet once more and this time pointed his arm at Jeremy. He was sweating and his skin was a sick greenish brown.

The green bolt of power went "Zzzzip" as it left Toad's arm and headed straight at Jeremy. Jeremy, seeing the bolt coming at him, turned to outrace it and ended up running inside one of the drain pipes. And like the drainpipes under most sinks, the pipe was curved.

Jeremy crawled as fast as he could through the pipe. The green lightning was right behind him. He saw the end of the pipe coming up and dove. Just as he hit the ground he looked up.

He was lying directly at Toad's green webbed feet.

Toad was looking down, grinning, his bloodshot eyes mad with victory. He took aim, pointed his arm and...

At that moment, the green bolt of lightning that had chased Jeremy through the curved drainpipe, came shooting out of the pipe's open end. Toad only had time to look up when the bolt hit him full in the chest. Toad was catapulted across the floor and skidded to a stop in a cloud of smoke.

Everything in Toad City stopped.

As the smoke cleared, Toad was sitting in the middle of the dirt floor, unchanged. His clothing was smoking. His chest was a little charred from the bolt of lightning, but otherwise he was the same old Toad. He got to his feet, looked at his arms and legs, touched his face, and let out a cry of victory.

"I AM INVINCIBLE!" he cried.

He started to laugh but stopped abruptly when his body began to twitch. He gasped as his feet and hands ballooned out into big hairy padded paws. The upper part of him, suddenly billowed into a round purple polka-dotted chest that continued up to his neck, ending in furry tufts. The change stopped at his head. Toad was stunned. His cheeks quivered. He began to sweat. His eyes a picture of terror. A green light started glowing in his toes and worked it's way up his body towards his head.

"Oh no! Stop! STOP!"

He tried to push the green light back down to his toes, but it kept coming until "POOF!", Toad's head was transformed into a tiny cross-eyed bird head with plumed feathers growing out of the crown. The creature that once was Toad, squawked unintelligently and stared into off into space.

Everyone in the shack moved closer to the creature to get a better look. Theodore approached the thing cautiously. The creature's tiny brain barely noticed him. It blinked it's one big eye while it's smaller eye wandered about the room.

A loud crackle of electricity caused all the heads to turn. A long charcoal-covered snake-like thing flashed with electricity like an electric eel, inching it's way across the floor. The crispy rattlesnake jerked and spurted, it's eyes blank as it jerkily squeezed through a crack in the shack wall and slithered away.

"The necklace!" Theodore shouted.

He hopped around frantically searching, while Maggie, Jeremy and Erin joined in. The residents of Toad's palace still didn't move. They didn't know what to do without Toad to direct them.

"Over here!" Maggie called.

Maggie was standing in back of the what-once-was-Toad creature. Beside the creature's feet was a freshly dug hole.

"The moles!" said Erin.

"If they're the ones who stole it the first time," said Maggie, "they're probably on their way back to…to…"

"My cousin, Archie," Theodore completed.

While the others were staring at the hole, the Raccoons crawled up onto the transformer that had been used to recharge the necklace. Slick grabbed one of the cables and glanced at Fatbottom. Fatbottom, in turn, grabbed the other cable and glanced back at Slick. They both got the same wicked idea.

Winkie scaled the wooden pole that had the electrical switchbox mounted on it. His one eye was twitching, but his two front teeth were sparkling inside a wide grin. He hooked the twine over the switch and climbed down with the rest of the twine in his teeth, finding a perch four or so feet off the ground.

Erin, standing beside Maggie and the rest, caught the movement of the Raccoons out of the corner of her eye. "Now what do they think they're doin' up there?"

Jeremy looked at the raccoons and shrugged.

"If we could understand them, we'd really be in trouble."

Danny climbed to the top of the platform and raised an arm. In a loud voice he addressed the residents of Toad City.

"My fellow citizens..." he began.

Slick and Fat Bottom strained as they stretched the cables far enough to hook them together.

"My friends and residents of Toad City...." Danny went on, as all heads turned to him. He was enjoying all the attention. "My comrades and I have successfully removed the tyrant, Toad, from office...so to speak. But what now, my friends? It looks like we're badly in need of a new management. Sooo... I'm offering my services as the new Mayor of Dumptown." He waved his hands as a signal for cheering, but none came, so he continued. "As for my policies, I believe in a loose governmental structure, food and employment for all, and a nice cushy residence for the Mayor. Nothing excessive just a little five bedroom flat..."

Slick yelled up to Winkie.

"HIT IT, MATE!!!"

Winkie jumped off of his perch with the twine tied to his ankle like he was bungee jumping. As his weight took up the slack in the twine, the twine pulled down the switch. Danny was so involved with his speech that he didn't notice.

"...I would be a benevolent leader, if I do say so myself. There'd be very light taxation....at least to start with, and…"

"THWACK!" went the cables as they pulsed with power from the transformer. Slick and Fatbottom dove for cover. Danny turned round just as the voltage hit the exposed wire. He yelled and jumped off of the platform. An explosion of sparks erupted in front of the platform and was growing larger. Jeremy grabbed Erin's hand.

"Run!" he yelled.

Everyone scattered as the surge of electricity changed from a hum to a rumble to a ROAR!. Within moments, Toad City was a mass of dancing bolts of electricity pulsing faster and faster until the roof blew off, sending a bouquet of sparks and bits of flaming debris into the night sky. Then, with an enormous "BOOM" the building blew to pieces as the transformer exploded.

CHAPTER TWENTY NINE

Yards away, Jeremy, Erin, Theodore and Maggie climbed a small heap of rubbish to watch Toad's empire disappear in sparks and flame. While the others watched, Theodore was staring at the moon. It was floating, like a yellow ball behind the pillar of billowy gray smoke.

"Almost full," Theodore said, sadly. 'My time is up. I've failed."

The others looked up at the moon too. They wanted to comfort their friend, but none of them had any comfort to give.

Meanwhile, four scorched figures climbed onto the top of another pile of garbage not far away. Their figures were outlined by the moon and by the display of sparks still spraying into the air from what was once Toad City. The four raccoons coughed. Their hair was still smoking.

"Wha' a party!" Slick blurted out, his hair black and sticking out in patches like a porcupine's.

"Never was there such drama!" said Fatbottom between coughs.

"F-f-f-f-ireworks and everything!" Winkie added.

Danny was coughing too and glared at the other three.

"You nits realize you ruined the most beautiful

speech of my life!" he pushed Slick and Winkie. They went head over heels down the pile. Danny then attacked Fatbottom and they wrestled as Slick and Winkie climbed back up again. Soon everyone was pushing and shoving everyone in a long moon-lit game of King of the Hill. A game which continued until the light of morning crept over the eastern hills.

CHAPTER THIRTY

At sunrise the next morning, smoke was still rising from the far side of Dumptown. Theodore was sitting on a broom handle resting his head on his hands, pushing the folds of his jowly face up around his eyes. Jeremy and Erin were sitting nearby to keep him company. But Theodore was too far away for anyone to keep him company. He was on Royal Pond. He was dreaming of that place he would never see again.

Maggie waddled over and sat down next to him. Many of the mice from Toad's palace were gathered around the King as well. As Theodore would have said, had he been his former self, they knew royalty when they saw it.

"You could always be King here?' Maggie said.

Theodore didn't look up.

"Well I don't know about you guys, but I'M going back!" said Jeremy stubbornly. "That necklace in the wrong hands could...well, we all know what it could do!"

"It's too late," Theodore said. "Tonight is the full moon. The Coronation. If I went back now I'd be put the dungeon forever."

"Do you think the moles could make it back that fast?" asked Erin.

"Probably," Maggie said.   "At least by late

afternoon."

"It's hopeless," said Theodore.

Jeremy got up and walked away kicking pebbles in frustration. Erin followed.

CHAPTER THIRTY ONE

Leaning against an old bicycle tire, Jeremy stared at the wispy trail of smoke far off in the distance.

"I'm sorry for him, the King," said Erin.

"It's just that we've come such a long way," said Jeremy.

"I know," she said. She looked at Jeremy and swallowed. This next part was difficult for her to say. She'd put it off all morning.

"Jeremy...I...I have to tell ya' that I'm...well, I'm proud to know ya'...and that's the truth." She waited for a reaction. None came. Jeremy didn't seem to hear her.

"It just doesn't make sense that we should come this far for nothing," he said absently.

"Jeremy?" said Erin, moving in front of him to get his full attention, "I said, I'm proud ta' know you and I... I... well I'm in love with ya'. There, I've said it!"

Jeremy nodded, but just kept talking to himself.

"Nothing's just 'impossible'. I mean, there's got to be something we're not thinking of."

Erin put her hands on her hips and gave him a look that would drill holes through steel.

"Are you listening to me?"

Jeremy blinked. His train of thought broken, he

finally noticed Erin.

"What's wrong?" he asked stupidly.

"What's wrong! Didn't ya' hear a thing I just said?"

"Yeah. No. I mean... about what?"

If Erin had been a volcano at that moment, red hot lava would be flowing out of her ears. Instead, she began ranting and raving, tossing her arms in the air, pacing back and forth, pointing or wagging her finger in Jeremy's face. Jeremy just stood there not understanding a thing she was saying. To Erin, this was an even greater crime.

"I pour out my heart and ya' pay no more attention to me than if it were nothin' at all! Ya' fly into my life, steal my heart away, and don't care this much when I tell ya' how I feel! Ya'...ya' save my life, fight braver than any mouse in ten thousand, and...and then... Well fine! Ya' won't see me makin' a fool out o' myself any longer!" She put her face menacingly in front of his. "Well say somethin'!" she demanded.

Jeremy opened his mouth, but nothing came out. She grabbed his vest, pulled him close and kissed him. Jeremy was stunned. Suddenly, his eyes got big and his face lit up.

"That's it!" he shouted, grabbing her arms. "That's it! That's it!" He took off at a run in the direction of Theodore. Leaving Erin stunned.

CHAPTER THIRTY TWO

Jeremy came running up the short hill where Theodore and Maggie were still sitting. Panting he said, "I know how to get there before the moles!"

Theodore hopped to his feet. "What? How?"

"We fly!" Jeremy said. He turned to Maggie. Maggie looked at her drooping wing which was made worse by last night's activity.

"You mean, Maggie?" Theodore asked. "Nonsense, that's out of the question. She's badly injured."

"Wait a minute now… Come ta' think of it, he might be right," Maggie said, "Don't know why I didn't think about it. No moles could dig or run or whatever they do, faster than I could fly."

"But Maggie, old girl," said Theodore sincerely, "you can't. Your wing!"

"The main thing is that I get…I mean that 'we', get that necklace before the full moon."

"It's our only chance, your highness!" Jeremy insisted.

Theodore looked gravely at Maggie's bent wing.

"Command me, Sire," said Maggie quietly.

Theodore took a deep breath and said, "Very well, Maggie. If you can, take us to Royal Pond!"

It was only then that Jeremy's brain translated the other things Erin had said.

"I love you?" he said.

"Well, I've grown very fond of you too, my friend," said Theodore, "but now is not the time..."

"She said "I love you," Jeremy said, and a stupid smile spread over his face. He took a step to go look for Erin, but Theodore dragged him back.

"No time to waste, dear boy! Come!" Theodore said.

A few minutes later, Jeremy and Theodore found some old window shutters and climbed up it like a ladder. Maggie moved underneath and together mouse and frog jumped on Maggie's downy back. Maggie decided on a trail that she would use as her runway. It was short, and at the end of the trail was an old tractor, but it was the flattest path.

"Stand back everyone!" Maggie told the surrounding onlookers. Mice, lizards, and weasels spread apart along the runway as Maggie tested her wings.

"Okay so far," she said to her passengers. "Ready?"

"Ready!" called Theodore from up on her back. She put her head down and began to run. Theodore and Jeremy held on to handfuls of feathers.

She got closer and closer to the end of the runway, and to the tractor, but she couldn't stop now. The rusted old tractor body was getting dangerously close. Still, on she ran, faster and faster. It was now or never. Theodore and Jeremy closed their eyes. A foot away from the old tractor body…Maggie took to the air.

Theodore and Jeremy cheered as Maggie circled the smoldering Toad City. Some of it's former citizens were waving. Jeremy saw Erin down below. She was not waving.

"Erin!" Jeremy shouted. He was suddenly horrified. "Oh no! What did I do!"

"What?" asked Theodore through the rushing wind.

Jeremy waved to Erin and yelled, "Me too! Erin!! Me too!!" Whether she heard him or not, he didn't know. They climbed higher and higher and in moments Erin was too small to see.

Maggie made a steep turn as mouse and frog hung on with all their strength. She headed toward the setting sun. Toward Royal Pond.

CHAPTER THIRTY THREE

It wasn't long before Maggie began to tire. She cleared another small cluster of pine trees. One wing was doing most of the work as she was gasping for air.

"I can't...stay up...any longer," she said.

She spiraled down awkwardly until she reached the ground with bad landing. Jeremy and Theodore were thrown off on the first bump. Jeremy bounced onto some moss covering the base of a pine tree. Theodore hit the moss too, but skidded into a stream just beyond. Maggie tumbled, rolling over and over until she finally came to a stop.

Theodore climbed out of the stream as Jeremy shook his head clearing his double vision.

"What a refreshing dip!" said Theodore.

Jeremy saw Maggie lying in some tall grass. Her body was heaving and her mouth was open, wheezing for more air. Jeremy was the first to reach her.

"Are you okay?"

Maggie groaned and said, "I can't (Pant, Pant) make it. You go on... leave me..."

"It's too far from here, Maggie," Jeremy said, patting her neck. "We'd never make it anyway."

"Besides," added Theodore, "we'd never leave you, dear girl."

Maggie's body heaved with every breath. Jeremy and Theodore decided to let her rest and walked over to the top of a rise that overlooked a vast canyon. The rise was actually a cliff . The stream fell off the cliff in a waterfall that seemed to change into a white powder near the bottom. Jeremy pointed to the canyon below.

"Over there, that's where Royal Pond should be."

"Too bad," said Theodore in a defeated tone, "I should have liked to have seen the moss of home once more."

"Then…let's go," came a voice from behind them.

Maggie, wobbly and weary, was motioning for them to climb back up on her back. "Come on."

"You can't, Maggie," Jeremy said kindly. "Your wing…it's not mended yet and it's just too far."

Maggie looked off into the distance for a moment, then back at Theodore and Jeremy.

"I always said I'd do anything for a friend…if I ever had one." She looked at the two of them. "Now I got two. So, come on. Besides, looks like it's downhill from here."

Theodore stared into her eyes for a brief instant and saw how serious she was.

"Very well, Margaret," Theodore said, patting her wing. "But only downhill."

She stretched out her good wing and the two climbed on board. As Maggie jumped off the cliff with the mouse and frog on her back, she repeated Theodore's words with each beat of her wings.

"Very well, Margaret," she whispered.

CHAPTER THIRTY FOUR

Archibald stretched his neck as Richfield fussed about, fluffing collar and straightening the red sash.

"I do so love fine clothing," Archibald said while he admired himself in the mirror. "Especially when it's on me."

"Clothes make the frog," Richfield assured him.

Archibald raised an eyebrow at Richfield, letting his monocle fall for more effect.

"Clothes make the frog... what?" Archibald asked. Richfield's eyes grew very large as he realized his mistake.

"Of course...uh, I mean, clothes make the frog, "Your Highness"," Richfield corrected. Archie smiled and gazed at himself in the mirror again.

There was a knock at the door, and the door began to open. Archibald watched in the mirror as a round face with big red lips appeared around the door. It was Gypsy.

"Oh sweetie, you look gorgeous!" Gypsy said as she entered the room.

"Good lord…" said Archibald without moving his lips.

Richfield, of course, had no trouble using HIS lips. He wrinkled his nose as if a foul smell had just entered the room.

"Oh. It's you," he said.

"What are you doing here?" asked Archibald. "I told you not to come. You could ruin everything."

"I got a right, ain't I?" asked Gypsy in a hurt little voice. "After all, I got to see wha' it's like to be a Lady of the Court so's I can act propuh' when you make me one."

Richfield snickered.

Gypsy gave him a murderous look.

"Why don't you find some nice bullfrog and seh-ull down," she said, and then patted her hair, as if talking to Richfield was enough to muss it.

"Nice clothes," Richfield said snidely. "Working at a circus now, are we?" Gypsy was about to clobber Richfield with her purse when Archibald stepped between them.

"Stop bickering both of you!" He turned back to the mirror and adjusted his tie. "Now," he said talking to Gypsy's reflection, "is there anything you NEED before you go?"

Gypsy stuck out her lower lip in a pout. "Well," she said, "I did run into those mole friends of yours."

Archie stopped adjusting his tie. A worried look came over him.

"And…"

"And," Gypsy continued, still pouting just in case he was looking. "They said to tell you they had a secret, and to meet 'em at the waterfall...that's all."

Archie scowled and looked out the window at the setting sun.

"The ceremony begins in an hour. What could those fools possibly want now--" Then his eyes brightened. "They couldn't have the necklace?" He swung around to Richfield. "Just think, Richfield, to wear the Necklace to the Coronation..."

"It would be frosting on the cake," said Richfield, slyly.

"But wha' about <u>me</u>?" Gypsy asked.

"YOU," said Archie, pointing a finger at her, "must return to the cabaret. If you're seen here now, no one would ever permit you into the Court. I'll take care of everything AFTER I am King. Now run along, and don't let anyone see you!"

This was clearly not the answer Gypsy had been hoping for. But, her desire for becoming a Lady of the Court was far too important to quibble over one silly Coronation. She gave Richfield one last sneer, and walked out of the room.

"You can't possibly be thinking of making that... that "riff-raff " a Lady of the Court?" Richfield said.

"Ah, Richfield..." Archibald began, slipping in his monocle, "have a bit more faith in your sovereign. Gypsy has been very useful. And at times, shall we say...a diversion. But that is quite all.... I'd no sooner make that trollop a Lady of the Court, then I would make YOU one."

Richfield suddenly got an odd look on his face. He started to daydream.

Gypsy pulled her ear away from the door outside the room. Eye make-up was running down her face from the tears. She lifted her head, gathered up what was left of her pride, and walked down the hallway.

CHAPTER THIRTY FIVE

Maggie was just barely clearing another grove of trees. She winced in pain.

"Maggie!" Jeremy called through the wind, "You have to stop!"

Maggie made one final flap of her wings and they began falling to the ground. Theodore was hanging on to one feather, his feet flying in mid-air. Jeremy slid backwards and was holding on to Maggie's tail feathers.

"Hold on, your Highness," Jeremy called.

With a spray of dirt and feathers, Maggie struck the ground, sending the mouse and frog sailing from her back. She tumbled end over end, finally rolling to a stop in a clump of brown grass. Her body was limp. Lifeless.

CHAPTER THIRTY SIX

Jeremy was the first to come to.

He found Theodore lying face-first in a patch of clover, dazed but unbroken. Jeremy helped him up.

"Are you okay?" Jeremy asked. Then they noticed the feathers Theodore was still holding in his clenched hand.

"Maggie!" they both cried and ran.

As they got close, they saw that Maggie's body was lying very still. Her neck was outstretched and her mouth was open. Her feet were sticking floppily in the air. Her eyes were closed.

"No!" cried Theodore, running to her. "Maggie! Maggie, my dear!" He came up next to her head and dropped to his knees. Jeremy put a hand on his shoulder.

"All because of me!" Theodore cried. "All my fault! I don't deserve to be King!"

"She wanted you to be King," spoke Jeremy softly. "You HAVE to be King now. Don't you see?"
Theodore looked up at him with a tear-streaked face.

"I suppose so..." he said.

Jeremy looked around.

"I know this place. Isn't the pond, just over there, over that knoll?"

"Yes," said Theodore, composing himself. "I must hurry. There may still be time!" He rose and looked at Jeremy.

"I think I'll stay, your Highness. I... I don't want her to be alone."

"Of course," said Theodore, nodding. "This is my responsibility from here on, my friend. Thank you."

Theodore hopped away, over the knoll, toward the pond.

CHAPTER THIRTY SEVEN

Beside the waterfall that flowed into the pond, Charlie and Irving paced back and forth. They were worried that the message they had given Gypsy had been too secret. They'd been having problems with secret plans lately. They were secretly thinking of giving them up.

Their fears were relieved when Archibald appeared through the reeds. Irving quickly hid the necklace behind his back.

"Well?" said Archibald impatiently. "What is it? I don't have much time."

"We got a secret," Charlie said.

"And…? What is it?" demanded Archibald.

"Well, it's," began Charlie and Irving clamped a hand over his mouth.

"If you tell him it won't be a secret anymore," Irving explained in Charlie's ear.

"Mmmm…you got a point there," Charlie agreed. Archibald was completely fed up. His head was visibly swelling because of the pressure. Both mole watched this and wished they could make their heads swell like that too.

"How do you do that?" Charlie asked.

"GET TO THE POINT YOU IDIOTS!" Archibald yelled, hopping up and down in frustration.

"Show him quick, before he blows up!" Charlie said.

From behind his back, Irving produced the glimmering silver necklace. Archibald's eyes got as big as saucers.

"The necklace!" he said in awe. "Finally! It's mine!" Archibald grabbed for the necklace, but Irving yanked his hand back.

"Promise first that you'll turn us into humans," he said.

"Certainly," said Archibald sincerely.

Irving held out the necklace and Archibald snatched it away. He grinned, tossing the necklace from hand to hand. Abruptly he stopped, held it tightly, positioned his feet, and made a hocus pocus gesture in the direction of the moles.

"Hmmm, what a shame, doesn't work. Should have turned you into humans. Oh well, perhaps you dropped it, or something. Got it wet. Either way it appears to be broken now. I feel terrible about the whole thing, really I do. After all the trouble you went to."

Charlie and Irving were more confused than normal.

"But…it's GOT power!" Charlie said.

"I'm afraid not," said Archibald, shaking his head. "You saw me try to change you. It didn't work at all. Just a silly old trinket now. But, I suppose I'll keep it for sentimental reasons."

The two moles were beginning to panic.

"No no no no! Toad put lightning in it!" said Irving. "Look it glows!!"

Archibald looked down at the necklace, and for the first time noticed it did indeed glow a brilliant green. He frowned.

"You mean... the legend is true? The necklace DOES have power?"

The moles nodded.

"This is too much! A Coronation and the power of the necklace restored! All in one day!" Archibald began to dance around the moles, delirious with joy. The moles watched the frog dance.

"Hey, he's not bad," Irving said to Charlie. Archibald was laughing on the point of tears. He had lived under the idea that being bad somehow had brought him bad luck. But here he was, a perfect villain, holding the one thing he had wanted most in the world.

"Ha ha! I don't believe it! I steal the throne from my spineless lump of a cousin, my dream come true, and here, on the day of my Coronation you bring me the Royal Necklace! Its power restored! WHO SAYS CRIME DOESN'T PAY!"

A booming voice came from above.

"WE DO!!!!"

Archibald jerked to a halt. He turned his head

slowly to the top of the waterfall. There, peering down at him was Lord Hopkins and the other Lords of the Court. But the frog standing between them all shocked Archibald the most.

It was Theodore Rivvit the Third.

"We've been looking for you, dear cousin," said Theodore calmly. "Fortunately we happened upon this informative young lady." Theodore moved aside and Gypsy walked to the edge of the cliff beside Lord Hopkins. She tickled Lord Hopkins under chin. He grumbled and turned a bit pink around the edges.

"We've heard everything, Duke Archibald," Lord Hopkins said. "You are a proper scoundrel! Thank goodness we found you out in time. Guards! Put that frog in irons!"

A division of frog guards marched down the rocky slope and surrounded Archibald.

"Stop!" cried Archibald. "All of you stop right where you are!" He held the necklace up in his hand.

"Wait!" Theodore yelled from above. The guards halted.

"Tell them, cousin! I have the Necklace! I won't hesitate to use it!"

"Do as he says!" Theodore ordered. The guards backed away. Archibald laughed triumphantly.

"So it's true after all!" he said. "The power of the

necklace HAS been restored! Who needs your paltry coronation now? I have power enough to rule the world!!" Sneering at them, Archibald spread the chain in order to place it over his head. He paused and looked at Theodore.

"My dear cousin... you've been a constant pain to me since your birth. You'll be the first one I get rid of. Not my last, I assure you!" He laughed and lowered the necklace.

Suddenly, from over the horizon, a dark shape swooped down at Archibald. Archibald ducked as the great shadow passed within inches and then angled up again into the sky. Archibald looked at his hands.

The necklace was gone. Theodore cheered!

"MAGGIE!!"

CHAPTER THIRTY EIGHT

With great difficulty, Maggie flapped her way over to large rock overlooking the pond. Her landing was rough, but she kept her balance. She looked battered and bloody. Her chest was heaving for breath. Her eyes were red and drooping from exhaustion, but they were fixed on the pond. Far off in the fading light, she could make out the shapes of ducks floating on the water.

Jeremy ran up next to Theodore, out of breath, and saw Maggie.

Maggie looked at the necklace. "No one'll ever call me ugly again," she said to herself. "No one!"

She looked at the ducks on the pond. All her memories came flooding back, replaying the sound of their laughter. A laughter she'd heard all her life.

Then another memory forced its way into her mind. The memory of Jeremy stroking her head.

Then the sound of laughter again, as she rolled in the mud to lure down the mud hawk.

Then Jeremy again saying, "Besides, I'll never leave you."

Then her reflection in the pond, as a little duckling, crying, and alone. That was it.

She slipped the necklace over her head and took off into the air.

Dark clouds were rolling in as she fly higher.

Within moments she was circling over one of the many bands of ducks that had been so cruel to her. They would never suspect what was about to happen to them. She would make them ugly. She would make them twisted and deformed. She would make them wish they'd never been born.

Mixed in with the rustling sound of her wings, she began to hear something else. Another memory forcing its way in. Two simple words that kept echoing inside her head. The voice was Theodore's. He was saying, "Very well, Margaret. Very well, Margaret."

Jeremy and Theodore watched Maggie circle over the Pond. It was over. The necklace was gone. The Lords of the Court knew this as well. Not having royal blood, all Maggie could do was destroy. And that would change her, even if she was good at the start, she wouldn't be the Maggie they once knew. Lord Brimbly faced Theodore's and bowed.

"Your Highness, you did all that could have been done..."

"Not quite enough, I'm afraid," sighed Theodore. "I have failed my subjects, Brimbly. All who live on Royal Pond. And caring for one's subjects is all a King is good for, really. Shame I didn't realize that before."

A shadow passed over head.

"Not surprising clouds would roll in," Jeremy thought. "Skies should be dark." Then he heard Theodore cry out.

"MAGGIE!" Theodore was hopping up and down, and so were some of the old Lords of the Court, though they had a harder time of it. Theodore waved his arms and hooped again, "Maggie, old girl!"

"Maggie!" Jeremy shouted, not believing his eyes.

Maggie circled lower and lower until she came to a clumsy skidding landing in a pool of water to one side of the waterfall. The Lords ran to her, but parted as Theodore approached. Maggie slowly paddled to shore. She stopped and looked at Theodore for a while. Then she dipped her head to the ground. The necklace slid down her neck and landed at Theodore's webbed feet.

"Probably look better on you," Maggie said to Theodore.

"Thank you, Maggie, my dear," said Theodore.

Down below the waterfall, Archibald was yelling and throwing a royal tantrum. The guards closed in around him.

"No! No! No! It's not fair, I tell you! I should be King. Me! Me! ME! It's my destiny! My fate!"

He pointed at the guards. "You can be my Royal Guard! Wouldn't that be nice? You'd have weekends off! Holiday pay! Free dental!"

The guards grabbed him. He tried to hop over them but they pulled him back down.

"Mumsie!!"

Theodore slipped the necklace over his head and as the power of the necklace surged through his royal blood, his body began to give off a dim greenish light. The Lords and onlookers all bowed without thinking.

"Your Majesty," said Lord Hopkins, bowing.

"Your Majesty..." repeated all those present. Even Jeremy and Maggie found themselves bowing.

"You may rise," said King Theodore.

Theodore walked to the edge of the cliff and looked down at his cousin Archibald.

"Release him!" Theodore told the guards.

The moon was climbing over the mountains and cast golden light on the water. The guards released Archibald. Archibald looked up nervously at Theodore.

"Because you are of Royal blood, by law I may not sentence you to death for your crimes. But neither can I banish you. I have witnessed the result of that myself, with Toad. Therefore, I sentence you to a fate you were so willing to inflict on everyone else."

Archibald's eyes bulged as Theodore lifted his arm and pointed his finger. A green lightning bolt shot from his finger and struck Archibald in the stomach. In the blink of an eye, his form began to shrink smaller and smaller until, what was once a frog, became a common pond fly.

"Oh noooo!" came the tiniest voice imaginable.

The fly, that was once Archibald, flew into the air, buzzing round and round and finally set course over the pond. Everywhere it flew, frog tongues shot into the air.

"Eeeek!" came the tiny voice of the fly, as dozens of frog tongues tried to snap him up.

The two moles, Charlie and Irving, were edging away from the waterfall as all this was going on. Suddenly though, they were aware that the attention had shifted in their direction. They dove for the ground and madly tried to dig their escape.

"Stop!" commanded Theodore.

The moles stopped digging, looked up at Theodore, and gave him a shy little wave. Just for an instant, they were both struck by the fact that the moonlight made Theodore look very much like the...Frog God.

A low thick growl came from behind Theodore. The big black bear was working his way down to the pond, as he did every night at this time. Theodore looked in the direction of the bear, then at the moles below.

"Since you have been so eager to become human, a form of animal we all disdain, and since I can no longer tolerate your presence here at Royal Pond, I will grant your wish."

The moles jumped for joy and threw their arms around each other.

"Humans!" cried Charlie.

"Humans!" cried Irving.

"Me first," said Charlie, spreading his arms and sticking out his chest. Irving pushed him aside exposing his own chest.

Theodore pointed his arm and a green flash struck both moles at once. When the smoke cleared, clinging to each other, were two naked human men.

Charlie and Irving examined each other. They leaped for joy again and danced round in circles.

"Money!!" shouted Irving.

"Cigars!" shouted Charlie.

"Toilets!" cried Irving.

"Fast food," cried Charlie. "And..."

A loud growl cut them short. Then another deeper growl. Charlie and Irving slowly turned around. The big black bear was standing on its hind legs a foot behind them.

"Aaaahhhh!" they both screamed.

The two naked humans ran for their lives with

the hungry bear close at their heels, snapping its vice-like jaws. As Charlie and Irving ran, their tender human feet seemed to step on every rock and sticker bush imaginable.

"Ouch!"

"Ooh!"

"Yipes!"

"Eeek!

"Yaooh!"

The screams of Charlie and Irving and the growls of the bear could be heard until they disappeared over a distant hill.

Two guards brought Richfield before Theodore and plopped him down onto his knees. Richfield put his hands together, pleading.

"Sire, I was forced! Blackmailed! It's all a hideous mistake!"

Theodore put out a hand to stop his whining.

"I am the one who made the hideous mistake by trusting you. But I will not use the power of the necklace on you. You're not worth it."

"Oh, thank you your Majesty, I--"

"Instead," continued Theodore, "I sentence you to hard labor for the rest of your days... in the Royal Laundry."

Richfield made a deep, horrified gasp.

"NO!" he screamed and crawled on his hands and knees towards Theodore. "Not that! Do you realize what laundry uniforms look like? Plaid smocks! Striped hats! Any fool knows you don't wear stripes with plaids! Please, Your Highness! Banish me, kill me, anything but not the laundry!!! P-P-PLEASE!!!!"

The guards carried him away still pleading and clawing at the ground.

Lord Hopkins cleared his throat and bowed.

"The celebration of the full moon is about to commence, your Highness. With all that has happened, I hope you will grace us with your presence?"

Theodore thought for a moment, then spoke.

"Yes. And I will also grace them with the presence of my friends, Jeremy the Mouse, and Maggie the Duck. Make their places ready. Oh, and one more thing, Lord Hopkins..."

Theodore drew Lord Hopkins aside as the guards lined up on either side of Jeremy and Maggie.

"I guess we're going to a Coronation," Jeremy said. Maggie shrugged as if she guessed so, too.

CHAPTER THIRTY EIGHT

The Coronation was a spectacular event. Firefly fireworks filled the air. Beautiful floats made of reeds and flowers and lilies covered the water in front of the Royal Palace. The entire Court was assembled. Fireflies sat on posts, brightly lighting the Courtyard, and the Court steps.

Jeremy and Maggie stood before Theodore, who was seated on his throne. All the residents of Royal Pond watched in awe. It was a spectacle unlike anything they had ever seen. And no one but frogs had ever been allowed to be before the King.

Theodore never dreamed he would actually enjoy this sort of thing. But he did. He began to see the pond as something more than it used to be. A kingdom filled with creatures, each having their own dreams, each having their own lives to live. He looked out at the thousands of frogs who had come from every end of the pond to watch the ceremony. It was the first time he ever truly felt like a King.

Theodore rose and put his hands up to silence the almost deafening croaking noise of the crowd.

"My people! At this time, I choose to honor two brave souls, to whom I, and Royal Pond owe a debt of gratitude. They championed your King on a great quest! They helped return the Royal Necklace to our kingdom. They risked their lives, and they deserve our thanks."

The pond resounded with applause. Theodore quieted them again as a sword was brought before him by a Palace Guard. Theodore took the sword and placed it on Jeremy's shoulder.

"To you, Jeremy, for your untold bravery, your true heart, your compassion, I bestow upon you the title of 'Knight'."

Theodore tapped Jeremy on each shoulder with the sword. A Paige approached carrying a beautiful silver sword on a pillow, which he presented to Jeremy.

"Rise, Sir Jeremy, Knight of Royal Pond."

Jeremy rose, bowed and took the sword in his hands. The crowd cheered.

"Thank you, Your Majesty," Jeremy said, running his hands along the handle of the new sword at his side.

"Will you stay here with us, Jeremy?" Theodore asked.

"I'd like to come back someday...but, right now I think there's someplace else, someone, waiting for me."

"Ah, of course," Theodore nodded, "your village. Your fiancée'."

"No, sire. Actually, I thought I'd go back to Dumptown. They'll be needing some law and order now that Toad's gone. And there's somebody there who... I left behind."

"Say no more, dear fellow. But remember you shall always have a home with us here."

"Thank you, your Majesty."

Jeremy bowed and backed away. Theodore turned to Maggie.

"Maggie the Duck...for your bravery, and your selflessness, I bestow upon you the title of 'Lady of the Court' and 'Knight'." Theodore tapped her on each shoulder. "From this day forward, all subjects of my realm shall bow when you pass by, in honor of the service you have done your King."

Maggie looked up at him and shook her head.

"I can't, your Majesty. I planned to steal the necklace all along. See...in case you haven't noticed, I'm kind o' homely and, it always bothered me. I never had anybody. But if I can have friends, even lookin' the way am, well, that's good enough for me. That's more than I ever thought I'd have."

Theodore said nothing. He simply nodded. Maggie rose and waddled over to the edge of the water. Jeremy ran to her and gave her a hug around the neck.

"Be careful with that wing for a while," Jeremy said, trying not to cry.

Maggie smiled.

"Fireflies, light her way!" shouted Theodore.

Fireflies flew in from all directions and formed a

ring around Maggie as she entered the water. She swam out into the pond as frogs from everywhere pushed aside lilies to let her through. Others simply bowed as she passed by. It was a wondrous sight. Maggie, gliding along the pond, surrounded by fireflies.

She passed by a group of ducks. Among them were the hillbilly ducks that had been so cruel to her weeks before. They all bowed as she passed. Except the duck with the red beak. He recognized Maggie.

"Hey, idn't that the same...?"

A wing slapped him on the back of the head and he went face first into the water.

"She IS a great lady," said Jeremy. "I don't care what she says." Theodore nodded in agreement. Jeremy sighed.

"We two are the only ones who see her the way she really is,. Beautiful." Theodore pondered this a moment, an idea brewing in his Kingly head. He looked at Jeremy and smiled. Jeremy seemed to read his mind.

"Oh, yeah," Jeremy said. "That'd be great."

Theodore smiled and nodded. He stretched out his arm in Maggie's direction and said softly, "So that everyone can see what we see. Behold, Lady Margaret of Royal Pond…"

Theodore's body began to glow. The glow gathered strength and flowed down his arm. The bolt of lightning silently crossed the water as the crowd looked on in disbelief. Just as silently the green bolt of lightning enveloped Maggie, surrounding her with a greenish haze that hovered there. As the greenish haze around her lifted, the duck within the firefly procession was gone.

Within the circle of fireflies another larger shape could be seen. Graceful, poised and stately. Even from a distance, everyone's breath halted as they gazed at the new figure. It was a beautiful black swan. Something no one on the Pond had never seen before.

Maggie didn't notice. She already felt beautiful. Loved. That made her seem even more lovely and graceful.

As the sun slowly began to push away the night, crickets made up a new song, and frogs joined in chorus. The song was of the quest for the Royal Necklace. It spoke of Toad, of the Duke of Lily, even of the moles, who were turned into humans. But mostly, it told of the Knights of Royal Pond, and how a frog became a King.

ABOUT THE AUTHOR

Gordon Goodman grew up on a cattle ranch, but was composing music and singing professionally by age sixteen. Within a few years he was a baritone soloist and recording artist with symphonies all over the world. A veteran professional actor and singer, he has performed dozens of roles for the professional stage or screen, working with legendary actors and iconic film composers. He has worked as a professional painter, sculptor, and illustrator and creates artwork for television development projects and for institutions of higher learning. He has written many plays, musicals, and books, has two Masters degrees, a Ph.D. in psychology, a black belt, is certified in hypnotherapy and artificial insemination for dairy animals, and is an expert in the field of performance anxiety in humans (no, not in dairy animals). In addition, he teaches psychology and sociology at a performing arts college in Southern California. He has two children. His wife, formerly with the Rockettes at Radio City, is a choreographer for the Walt Disney Company. Gordon has received special commendations from both the California State Senate and the California State Assembly for his contributions to the arts.

www.ingramcontent.com/pod-product-compliance
Lightning Source LLC
Chambersburg PA
CBHW070702280626
47159CB00022B/1771